Sanibel's
Secret Bank

by

W. C. Highfield

To my son, *Bryan,*
who sparked my interest
in secret societies

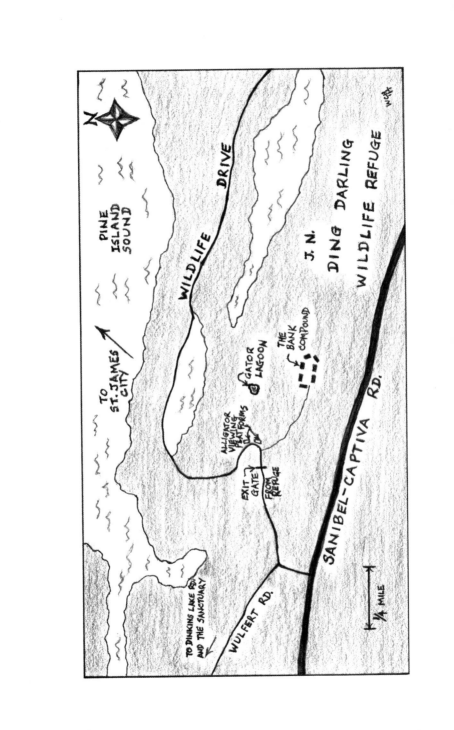

1

Mosquitoes feasted on me as I crept through tangled mangroves in the muggy August nighttime. The guiding beacon on my trek through the J. N. "Ding" Darling National Wildlife Refuge was a faint, shimmering glow of distant light reflecting off overhanging foliage. Muted, rhythmic drumming also helped direct the way. My body poured sweat and my heart raced, anxious and apprehensive. Pressing ahead, the flickering radiance brightened. Approaching what appeared to be the boundary of a cleared area in the subtropical underbrush, an acrid burning odor grew stronger and the drumming ceased.

With quiet caution, I parted branches of gnarled mangroves and viewed the source of light and smell. In a carved-out semi-circle, flaming torches lined the perimeter and blazed with intensity. The beams from their fire bounced on an elevated canopy of black fabric. The bright illumination in the surrounding darkness was mesmerizing, but the source of my interest was the group of individuals standing in the clearing.

Adorned in multi-colored, ceremonial mesh robes, the upper echelon management team of The Bank was assembled. Recognizing practically everyone in the gathering, and knowing their positions in the company, I realized the varied colors of the robes designated differing levels of authority in the executive hierarchy. The thin garments were an assortment of blues, greens, and browns.

Although I'd worked at The Bank for almost two years, the entire scene was far beyond anything I had ever witnessed. Adjacent to the cluster of six or seven male executives, a squad of uniformed security guards stood at attention. At their forefront, the stoic Webb Dunn maintained an authoritative stance. As Security Director of The Bank, Dunn commanded respect from all.

A low stage was at the head of the assembly. Above the raised platform, a symbolic sphere of the sun stood out against the surrounding blackness. The sun's distinct shape with emerging points seemed strangely familiar to me. But I was too caught up with the tension of the moment to give it a second thought.

On one side of what seemed more like an altar than a stage, a lone drummer was positioned. With the drummer's single clang of a bronze bell, the President and Chief Executive Officer of The Bank, Lucien Farr, approached the podium. He was attired in a bright yellow cape-like covering. The lightweight nature of the robe caused it to flow behind him as he moved. Although he is a less than average-sized man, Farr's presence is a great deal larger than his stature. His immediate assistant, Ava Branstein, followed. Robed in an orange color, she took a position on Farr's flank. Branstein, too, is small in height, but on the stout side. Upon reaching the lectern, Farr stood with his head bowed in silence for an extended moment before addressing the group.

"Fraternal Members, your implicit loyalty is an expectation that is the lifeblood of The Bank. Each of you has taken a vow of secrecy, along with a pledge of obedience, in declaring your commitment to the singular cause of our brotherhood. Your compliance is the foundation of your service. However, we are gathered here tonight due to an unfortunate heresy that has been committed within our organization."

Not a word was uttered by the group of high-level managers, but they stole wide-eyed glances from one another.

After another long pause, Farr continued, "A breach has been detected in the secure nature of our information systems. We have traced this breach to the Assistant Manager of the Data Processing Department." Gesturing toward the security detail, he raised his voice, booming, "Fraternal Members, I give you Tyler Morrison."

Webb Dunn turned back to the security detail and made an abrupt arm motion. The ranks parted and a blindfolded Tyler Morrison was brought forward a few steps, grasped at the arms by two broad-shouldered guards. Morrison's hands were secured behind his back. He was wearing business-casual clothing, which is the daily standard at The Bank. Although the costumed management team remained silent, their undivided attention, and mine, was riveted on the junior supervisor who was a well-liked co-worker. I had only interacted with him on several occasions but found him to be friendly and personable. What I was seeing and hearing seemed beyond belief. My insides were churning.

Farr spoke again, saying, "The particular specifics regarding the violation which has been committed are irrelevant. But I want to be exceedingly clear—it is an offense that will not be tolerated in our midst. And, therefore, appropriate punishment must be meted out. Bring Mr. Morrison before me."

My chest heaved in a fretful struggle for breath as Morrison was escorted to a position directly in front of, and below, Farr. Several times I wiped away the flow of sweat stinging my eyes. No doubt, mosquitoes were devouring my sopping body, but that discomfort was ignored.

One of the guards removed the blindfold from the defendant as Lucien Farr spoke again. "Mr. Morrison, you have disobeyed the doctrine and principle of secrecy upon which The Bank is established. Obedience to this code is not an option. For this most severe transgression, you must receive the ultimate punishment."

Morrison called out, "But I—"

"Silence," bellowed Farr.

Tyler Morrison began again but, before he could barely utter a word, one of the guards smacked a strip of duct tape across his mouth, silencing him.

"Fraternal Members," continued Farr, gesturing, "to my right is the Gator Lagoon, with which I believe you are all familiar."

Elevated spotlights circling a roughly half-acre shallow pond were switched on, exposing thick mangroves bordering the back and side portions of the murky body of water. On several scattered rock formations in and near the lagoon, mature alligators lay motionless.

With a stern voice, Farr said, "Please guide the disloyal infidel to his final destination on this earth."

Morrison resisted, but it was no use. The brawny guards virtually dragged his struggling body to the edge of the lagoon. In a swift series of moves, the guards cut the plastic ties from Morrison's hands and ripped the duct tape from his mouth. With the help of two others in the security detail, he was then flung headlong into the pond. While still airborne, Tyler Morrison cried out a terrified and sickening howl. As his body hit the water, alligators on rocks, and others in the brackish water, immediately converged on their flailing prey. What followed was fierce, violent thrashing in the low-lying lagoon. Morrison was quick to thrust the upper part of his body into the air, letting out a horrifying scream. But in an instant he was yanked back below the surface. The splashing, forceful flurry gradually subsided and then stopped. The surface of the water soon displayed a floating and ever-growing scarlet film. It was a gruesome ordeal lasting mere moments, but seeming like long hours.

I turned back from the scene and dry-heaved several times, leaving a burning bile in the back of my throat. It was the most grisly and awful thing I had ever seen, or could have ever imagined. My heart was pounding out of my chest, and I was shaking beyond control. Never before had I felt such terror.

My overriding instincts were basic—survival and escape.

Through the thick network of mangroves, I began to backtrack the path I had used to arrive at my spot, as much as was possible in near-darkness. I tried to be quiet, but several small branches were definitely snapped in my urgency to get away. I was hoping like mad I wasn't making enough noise to draw the attention of the security guards. It was a teetering tightrope balance of hushed, careful movement and outright, fearful flight.

I'd only gone maybe a dozen paces and had reached an opening in the quagmire of branches when a strong hand gripped across my mouth and I was tripped face-first to the ground. A bulky body landed on my back with a thump. "Shhhh, be quiet," a man's raspy voice whispered into my ear. "I'm not gonna hurt you. Just be quiet when I let you up."

Due to the combination of my frantic pulse and the fact that the wind had been knocked out of me, I was in no condition to speak anyway. The man came off of my back and pulled me to a sitting position.

"Now, what the hell are you doing out here tonight?" he whispered. "You want to end up like that poor bastard just did?"

I offered a weak wave of my hand and a shake of my head to delay any reply. I could just make out the shadowy outline of the husky man's bearded face and ruddy complexion. But what I could see clearly in the dim glimmer of light from the torches was a powerful, piercing look in his eyes.

"Listen," he said in a deep, gravelly voice, "I'm not gonna mince words with you, chum. You stay right with me, and do what I do, and maybe the two of us will get out of here in one piece. Got it?"

I was still gasping for air as I nodded in appreciative acceptance. The whole nightmare had exasperated me to the point where I was all set to follow him, without delay, to wherever he wanted to lead me.

"Let's go," he whispered, pulling me to my feet.

As we burrowed through the maze of mangroves for fifteen minutes or more, I stayed as close as possible to the burly man. Even though he was heavily built, he moved without difficulty through tight openings with stealth aggressiveness. Although I struggled to keep up with his brisk pace, I continued to be energized with the anxious rush of adrenaline.

When we reached an opening in the network of abundant undergrowth, a half-moon had risen, which shed light on a tributary of slow-moving water. The man motioned for me to stop as he leaned down and removed several mangrove branches covering a two-seat kayak. Sliding the limbs into the underbrush, he said in a low voice, "I suggest you hitch a ride with me, chum. Get in front and grab a paddle."

He launched the kayak from the water's edge, hopped in behind me, and we got underway in silence. In the dimly-lit surroundings I could just make out the shimmer of moonlight on the surface of the moving current of water. I paddled, but my companion was the one supplying most of the forward propulsion and all of the bearing. I had no idea what our destination was, and I didn't care.

As we neared what looked to be a large opening in the meandering waterway, my travel partner broke the silence. "Hold up there, chum, we're pulling over. I have it. Keep your head down."

I bent down and shielded branches away with my paddle as he guided the kayak through a cover of hanging seagrapes and mangroves. He brought the kayak up next to a small fishing boat anchored under the umbrella of foliage. We boarded the boat and he secured the kayak to the stern with a length of line. Using a pole, and with grunting effort, he pushed us off and back out of the overhanging branches. The captain started the outboard motor and, at low torque and sound, we were slowly thrust ahead.

We emerged into a large body of water that even in near-darkness I immediately recognized as Pine Island Sound. In the distance to our right, the moon's beam cast a faint silhouette of the tall bridge on the Sanibel Causeway. Straight ahead was the dim light of St. James City. After we had gone maybe a hundred yards, the skipper of our modestly-sized craft spoke.

"So, now tell me," he said, "what the hell were you doing back there tonight?"

"Well," I said, "I, uh, work…there. You know about The Bank?"

"Yeah, I know about The Bank." His raspy voice made his speech seem like he had just gargled with shards of broken glass in his throat. "Guess I know too much and not enough about The Bank at the same time. But that's a story for later. I'm always interested in coming across anything new. Why don't you go ahead and tell me your story, chum. Just pretend I don't know squat. For starters, what's your name?"

I hesitated for a minute, knowing that talking about The Bank to an outsider was taboo. But as we continued forward at low speed in the darkness, I decided the code of silence didn't mean much to me anymore. After all, here was the guy who had safely led me out of what would have been big trouble if I'd been caught spying. Maybe even saved me from a death sentence in the Gator Lagoon if I had somehow bungled my escape because I was scared and reckless.

"My name's Ben. How about you?"

"Garth. Garth Milner."

I paused again and finally continued, "And I was there tonight because I'm worried about some people I know at The Bank. I was just trying to find out more information about what's been happening lately."

"Well," he said, "you sure as hell got an adult dose of information. Go on. And start from the beginning. How long have you been there?"

"Coming up on two years," I said. "It's my first job since I graduated from college. I got the job because my father is Director of Facilities for The Bank, which means he's in charge of all of the buildings and their related services. I work in his department. I'm sure glad he wasn't back there at that scene."

"So there's a little nepotism going on with the hiring?"

"Exactly," I said. "That's the way it is at The Bank. Practically everybody is related in some way to someone else who was working there before them."

"Makes for a tight-knit group, huh?"

"Absolutely," I said. "It's a very selective process. And it makes it easier to keep everything regarding the secret nature of the operation under wraps."

"You're worried about somebody you know?" he said.

"Yeah, I've, uh, sort of been seeing this girl who works in data processing at The Bank. She told me, without a lot of detail, there was a shake-up coming. And it had to do with her office. I was back there because I wanted to see what was going on."

"Okay, there, Ben," he said. "Hold that thought until we get to my place. We can make it a lot faster if I fire this thing up. No worries about making noise now that we're out here in open water."

Garth had waited until we were well away from the back side of the refuge to increase the speed of the outboard. We accelerated forward at high torque. What a refreshing feeling it was to have a strong breeze blowing across my body. The discomfort from the sweat, the mosquito bites, and the scratches on my hands and arms from mangrove branches seemed to disappear.

Even with the loud din of the motor, there

was something settling about our fifteen or twenty-minute trip in the night air across the Sound. As I looked upward at the lightshow of sparkling stars in the cloudless sky, I calmed down several degrees from the anxiety of the very recent and very agonizing experience. I was just glad to be alive. Although I didn't know anything about Garth, there was an aura of safety about him. It made me feel as though he would be a good person to be with if there was ever any kind of trouble. I'd already had the benefit of that, firsthand.

2

When we reached St. James City, Garth cut the motor back, steered us left and then turned right at the second canal. At no-wake speed, we passed only a handful of houses lining both sides of the canal when he rotated the boat to a perfect dockage at the seawall. Completed with such casual and confident ease, it made me imagine he could have done it in his sleep.

After Garth secured the boat, we walked to his house across a short back yard of crushed shells. The house was a small A-frame style, looking more suited for the mountains of upstate New York than a fishing village in Southwest Florida. But even for the brief time I had been with him, it was easy to figure Garth was a free spirit. In that way, the uncommon house design seemed a perfect fit.

After we entered the back door, and Garth turned on several lights, I got my first clear look at him. The outside of his body was as rough and rugged as his voice. He had a sturdy barrel-like shape, and several faded tattoos on his chunky, sunburned forearms. In addition to his thick auburn beard, he wore his long sandy-colored hair in a ponytail, which stuck out from the back of his tan fishing cap. The wrinkled crow's-feet at the corners of both eyes confirmed that the sun had taken its toll on his exposed skin. It appeared he led an active outdoor life.

"Have a seat, chum," Garth said, pointing at the kitchen table. "I mean, Ben. Don't mind me, I call everybody chum. How 'bout a cold beer?"

"That sounds great," I said. "I could sure use it."

"Well, you're in luck," he said, opening the refrigerator. "I just picked up a case today."

After Garth uncapped the beers on an old-fashioned bottle opener attached to the side of a kitchen cabinet, he turned on the radio. "Hope you don't mind classical," he said. "I listen to it most of the time."

"Classical music is fine with me." I would never have chosen classical, but I sure didn't care one bit. He could play anything he wanted. It just struck me as funny he liked that type of music. It was a case of the book not seeming to fit the cover.

"I either listen to classical or the scanner," he said, smiling. "So I can choose between settling down and chilling out with the music, or I can go completely the other way and get juiced up listening to the police, fire, and marine activity. If I have the classical music and the scanner on at the same time it makes me go sideways."

As we toasted our bottles, Garth said, "Here's to being alive."

"Indeed it is," I said. We each had taken a few hearty gulps when I decided to turn the tables on my host. "So, here's a question for you, Garth. What were *you* doing in the refuge tonight?"

"I had a feeling you might ask that," he said. "I'm a contractor for the Florida Fish and Wildlife Conservation Commission. Long name, huh? I freelance different projects for them like alligator counts, bald eagle counts, manatee counts, you name it. Mostly in the area of Pine Island Sound. I'm real good at counting. Well, the last few nights I've been out on the water just to relax for a while. But I do keep my eye on the back of Ding Darling for another reason. Tonight as it was getting dark, I noticed a soft glimmer coming out of the refuge. Practically nobody would ever have noticed it, especially from a distance. There was that canopy over the top of the meeting area, but some faint light did trickle through the mangroves. When you've been out on the water as much as I have, with a fair amount of it at night, you pick up on anything that's even slightly different."

"So," I said, "what's the other reason?"

"Let's have another cold one first," said Garth as he got up and went to the refrigerator. When he swung the door wide open, I noticed the contents consisted of a gallon of milk, a large jug of orange juice, and a carton of eggs…plus the case of beer we were starting to do some damage on. It was funny that the refrigerator at the house I rented with two other guys had basically the same kinds of provisions. The main difference being Garth's was much cleaner inside.

We drank our beers without talking. I used the quiet time to glance around the inside of his house. It was basically just one oversized room with a kitchenette at one end and a living area at the other. There was an open door in between to what looked like a small bathroom. A spiral staircase near the front door led to a narrow loft. Window air-conditioners were running at the front and back of the house. With the A-frame design, the windowless side walls of stained wood planking vaulted on both sides to a peak of maybe twenty-five feet. If there had been a fireplace, it would have made for a cozy setting to look out over a hilly blanket of northern snow. But here it was on a canal in St. James City on Pine Island. The comfy feel of the house made me a whole lot more at ease than I had been previously.

"Let's go again, chum," said Garth as he opened two more bottles. I could do my share of beer drinking, but for the second time I had to finish off several big gulps to stay with Garth's pace. It certainly wasn't an unpleasant task, though. The cold brew went down just fine.

14

Garth plopped back down on the kitchen chair and stared straight through the middle of my eyes to the back of my head. Sitting beneath the overhead kitchen light, he had an even more intense look than I had seen earlier in the near-darkness of the refuge. "My uncle, who was only five years older than me, worked at Ding Darling as a ranger. He had nothing to do with The Bank. He worked for the refuge, plain and simple. Well, since you work there, I'm sure you are well aware that the section where the buildings are is off limits to everybody—refuge rangers included."

"Yeah," I said, nodding. "Everyone uses the standard cover-up line that it's an isolated area where sensitive wildlife research is being conducted. Nobody on the outside, or even anyone working at Ding Darling, is supposed to know what it is really about."

"That's what I've gathered," said Garth. "About six months ago, my uncle got curious about what was going on, so he started nosing around. He told me something seemed odd about what was happening with the extra security, but couldn't put his finger on it. He located the building compound and had done a little surveillance. Told me he was planning on keeping an eye on it, and that he'd let me know what he found out. Next thing I know, he went missing a couple of days later during his afternoon shift. Never came back to the rangers' office.

"Then it got written off by the Ding Darling people and the cops. They made it out like he must have been walking in the refuge and a gator got hold of him. And that was the end of that. I know it can happen with gators grabbing people. You read about it in the paper every now and then. But my Uncle Nate had been a ranger for almost twenty years and had a good head on his shoulders. Plus, he was strong as an ox. He didn't get pulled down and taken away by any goddamn alligator.

"I feel for sure he was tossed into that lagoon like what happened tonight. He was snooping where he shouldn't have been and he paid the price. He probably wasn't nosing around anywhere near where he ended up. I'm saying he was taken there. The Bank complex is far enough away in the refuge that the bullshit cover for their operation worked out. They're slick, but I guess you already know that."

"There is a ton of security," I said. "I know the secrecy within The Bank is solid, but I didn't know any of this kind of stuff went on. Like I told you before, I was there tonight because I'd been told by the girl I mentioned to you that there might be some special ceremony, and I was curious to see it. I sure didn't expect anything even close to what happened."

"Yeah," said Garth, "and did you happen to notice they cut the plastic ties off his hands and took the duct tape off his mouth? If and when some remains of him are found, nothing looks fishy. Must have gotten pulled in by the gators is what it will look like."

"And the clothes he had on," I said, "would be what he'd normally wear at work."

"He just went out for a walk during the day

and never made it back," said Garth, with a wry smile.

I shook my head and took a deep breath. I knew the whole business aspect of The Bank was a secure operation, but all of a sudden it seemed like I didn't really know what type of company I was working for.

"So, how do you think they'll get the meeting area fixed up?" said Garth. "It's not far from the alligator viewing platforms off Wildlife Drive."

"I'm sure that won't be a problem," I said. "Things get done at The Bank like it was yesterday. I know, since I work in facilities management. After that gathering disperses, I bet the security guards will break everything down, canopy and all, and take it away. The light poles around the pond, the electric lines, and whatever quiet-running generators providing the power will all disappear. They might even bring in vegetation to plant in the open area. In no time everything will be back to looking as natural as everywhere else in the refuge. That's the way it happens with anything at The Bank. Bing, bang, boom—job done quickly and job done perfectly. Like it never happened."

It was difficult to get a handle on what I *didn't* know about The Bank. I'd had no involvement with the inner workings of the financial end of the business. I didn't care about that. I was concerned with the buildings and their services. But now it was hitting me that I was naïve to a whole deeper layer of power and concealment. The reality of it was tough to swallow.

Garth called over his shoulder as he opened two more beers, "Now, what's the deal with you, chum? Are you going to be missed from where you're supposed to be?"

"It had crossed my mind," I said, "and the answer is no. I live with two other guys who work at The Bank. We rent a house together on Sanibel. And from time to time it would not be unusual if one or more of us might be crashing elsewhere, especially on a Friday night. We all agree there's no sense taking a chance on driving after a bunch of beers."

"But what about your car? Is it parked at the complex?"

"Yeah," I said, "it is. But that's not out of the ordinary, either. Sometimes people might go out together after work and then carpool the next day. Even though tomorrow is Saturday, it's fine. In the morning if you can just get me near some point on Wildlife Drive, I'll take a run back to my car for some exercise. I'm wearing sneakers, and I'll just cut off these long pants and make them shorts. Had to wear long ones for climbing through those mangroves."

"Yup," Garth said as he lowered his head a bit and got a more distant look in his eye. After a pause he said, "The whole deal with my uncle eats at me every day. Can't get my mind off of him for any big length of time. Makes my blood sort of boil."

He looked off to the side for a moment and continued, "I do see my aunt every now and then, mostly on special occasions. She lives in Fort Myers. My three cousins are all in their twenties. They are probably close to your age, plus or minus. It's a little odd that I'm twenty-five or so years older. Almost think of them as my niece and two nephews."

After a couple more beers, Garth decided we ought to call it a night. He put the last empty bottles in the recycle bin out on the back deck. He came in and pointed to the couch saying, "That's your bed tonight, chum. I sleep up in the loft. I'll leave the light on over the sink so you can make it to the bathroom when you have to get up and pee. I've got a container up next to my bed for that particular necessity. And I like to leave the classical music on low volume overnight. Helps create some soothing background sound. Here's a card with my phone number in case you ever want to get in touch. Something tells me we're going to meet up again. But let's hope it's under better circumstances. See you in the morning."

"Night, Garth," I said, "and thanks for everything."

I stretched out on the sofa but I was still keyed up from the evening's events. The multiple beers and the quiet music helped, though. To get my mind off of the earlier ordeal, I glanced around the dimly-lit room. Garth had some interesting belongings. There were mounted fish of various types, photographs of previous catches, several nautical maps, and fishing magazines decorating the lower level of the house. My host was certainly an outdoorsman if there ever was one.

I pulled Garth's card out of my pocket and held it up close so I could read it. There was a prominent seal in one corner of the Florida Fish and Wildlife Conservation Commission. Garth had been right; it was a long name. In the middle it said, Garth L. Milner, with the title, Consultant. His phone number and address were in the lower corner. Not wanting to take any chance on losing it, I buttoned it in my back pants' pocket.

I put my head back and thought about what a transition the night had been. It was hard to believe I'd started out on foot at dusk, snaked my way through the mangroves of Ding Darling, only to end up across Pine Island Sound in a stranger's house in St. James City. The best part was I had now reached the point where Garth didn't seem like a stranger to me at all.

3

I awoke to the sound of Garth rattling around the kitchen. The rich smell of coffee filled the house. It was just barely light but, in short order, I perked up with a renewed sense of energy. I borrowed a pair of scissors and proceeded to make shorts out of my khaki slacks. I also wrote my name and cell phone number on a pad of paper on the kitchen counter. Garth was much less talkative than the night before, so I followed suit.

After bananas and muffins, washed down with coffee, we were back in his boat and on our way. Garth even brought along a thermos of coffee and foam cups for our voyage across the Sound. It was invigorating to cruise along on smooth, glassy water in the early daylight. It provided a far different perspective than the boat ride the night before. The anxiousness and uncertainty of what lay ahead were still in my mind, but I felt strengthened and revitalized. I felt alive, and it was a good feeling.

Garth maneuvered us near the northern edge of the refuge, anchored the boat, and we proceeded to paddle his kayak through several tributaries where motorized boating is prohibited. When we reached a spot near Wildlife Drive, he let me out and we said our goodbyes, along with a firm handshake. It felt as though I was shaking his two hands put together as one. The fingers and palm of Garth's hand were that thick and strong. There was an unmistakable straightforward and down-to-earth honesty in Garth that was apparent when he looked me in the eye. I felt sure I would be seeing him again at some point. In a very short period of time, I had made a friend and a confidant.

During my run along the crushed stone drive in the steamy morning air, a squadron of ten or twelve white ibis streaked in formation low overhead. A barely audible swooshing sound from flapping wings was the only indication of their presence. The distraction by the cluster of ibis interrupted me from reflecting back on the circumstances that had led to my investigative journey the night before. I wanted to sort out, and try to put in order, my piecemeal laundry list of information about The Bank....

The one-story buildings in The Bank complex were built in the autumn of 2004. The work occurred in the months shortly after Hurricane Charley barreled through in August of that year. Charley caused major damage to most of Sanibel Island, and practically wiped Captiva, just to the north, off the map.

The reconstruction process taking place on the island after the storm set up perfect circumstances for the completion of the project. Virtually every structure on Sanibel required some type of repair, and in some cases necessitated rebuilding altogether. With building material delivery trucks and construction vehicles flocking to the island, no specific notice of the additional activity was taken by residents.

How The Bank managed to annex the several-acre plot in the J. N. "Ding" Darling National Wildlife Refuge is beyond my comprehension. But knowing how The Bank operates in general, I feel certain some manipulated misinformation, financial leveraging, or even strong-arm tactics, influenced the arrangement.

To make the location easily accessible but still controlled, the entrance trail into The Bank's compound is off Wildlife Drive. The drive is a one-way road that meanders for four miles through pristine natural surroundings. The entry point to get to the compound is covered with moveable foliage screens and is very close to where the drive exits the refuge.

Bank employees access the compound in reverse fashion. We enter Wildlife Drive in the opposite direction where there is a motion-controlled sliding gate that opens for visitors to leave. We use remote transponders to open the gate. When Wildlife Drive is available to park visitors, security guards of The Bank set up a brief stop to any approaching tourist traffic at one of the previous bends on Wildlife Drive. This allows employees to come and go unseen into the facility by way of the normal refuge exit.

The system works because bank guards wear uniforms similar to actual Ding Darling park rangers. Visitors traveling the drive who are stopped are not alerted to anything unusual for the short delay. And to refuge employees, the security personnel of The Bank are thought of as merely private rangers of the special research area with whom interaction is strictly prohibited. I had recognized most of the security squad the night before as being in this group.

The seven-building compound on The Bank grounds is camouflaged to aircraft by a state-of-the-art mesh fabric, which is suspended in patchwork fashion about thirty feet above ground level. Large sections of the fabric hang above all of the buildings, parking, and walkways of the complex. The mesh is a high-tech version of the one-way coverings on windows of public buses—it can be seen through from the ground but not from the sky. Looking upward from the facility, there is just slightly filtered daylight overhead. The view of the sky is nearly clear both day and night. But from above, the covering appears identical to the mangroves throughout the bulk of the refuge. The Bank goes to great lengths to make certain all aspects of secrecy are in place.

At first glance, the hierarchy at The Bank might seem similar to any other male-dominated company. But a difference persists. Not only are all of the upper-level managers men, they are universally indoctrinated into the belief of archaic notions concerning the proper sphere for women. Besides Ava Branstein, there are other women who are employed by The Bank, but in practically every case their roles are significantly inferior to men.

Beyond that inequality, there is a certain unique fraternity atmosphere existing in the higher management echelon. But it is unlike a true fraternity where members freely associate as equals for a mutually beneficial purpose. Within The Bank, there is a clearly defined chain of command carrying with it one inflexible guiding principle—the pursuit and accumulation of money, and yet more money, at any cost.

This philosophy permeates the ranks of upper management and, at the same time, drives the ambition of those lower on the company ladder. The entire culture is one of a sealed, secretive brotherhood intent on acquiring an incomprehensible amount of wealth. Overall, the universal policy is simple—do your job, do it efficiently, keep the secret, and you will be paid well. Very, very well.

My father was hired at The Bank a few years after the complex was built. He knew the inner circle of leadership because he was the facilities manager of the high-rise outside of Philadelphia where the core players got their start as an investment firm. My dad once told me that after a few years in the refuge, Farr decided there was a need for a manager to be solely responsible for the buildings. The Bank had grown to that point. I had limited knowledge of why my father decided to make the change, but I was fairly sure it had to do with a significant increase in salary

My mom and dad moved to Sanibel when I was a freshman at the University of Pennsylvania. During my college years, I really didn't spend much time with them here. I continued to work a summer job in construction that I had first gotten while still in high school. My parents realized I could earn far more up north with a summer job than I ever could on Sanibel. Being a bartender or a waiter would be almost the only options for me here. And I sure wasn't cut out for either of those. Plus, by staying with the same job, I was learning many aspects of construction in working my way up with a successful general contractor....

I was soaked in sweat by the time I got back to the complex. Along the way it occurred to me that a shower was going to feel mighty fine when I got home. Between the previous evening's activities and the morning run in humid conditions, I was not feeling as though I had any degree of freshness about me. I didn't mind the exercise, but I did have quite a thirst. I was sure the beers and the morning coffee hadn't helped with the dehydration issue.

I encountered two guards at the entrance of The Bank on Wildlife Drive. Having them recognize me as a member of the staff was no problem. The total number of employees, including security, was no more than roughly sixty or seventy. Everyone was trained to be at least visually familiar with co-workers. In many cases, that was as far as it went. The guards may well have thought I took a long run to get back to my car on the morning after a festive Friday evening happy hour. There were a few other cars in the parking area, which wasn't unusual on weekends. The incentive to excel in the investment section of the company drove many employees, especially younger ones, to work a ridiculous number of hours per week. Some pressed it beyond reasonable limits of what the mind and body could endure.

I retrieved my Jeep and made the short drive to the house on Dinkins Lake Road that I shared with two co-workers, Frankie and Seth. I drove out the exit of the refuge and, after a few hundred yards, made a right on Wulfert Road. On the ride up to Dinkins Lake Road, I waved to Frankie who was on his way out in his hotshot yellow Camaro SS. He's a very serious motorhead when it comes to cars.

Frankie's full name is Franklin Evans, Jr. His father is the head of transportation and waste management at The Bank. Frankie started out in the data processing department about a year ago just after he graduated early from Edison State College in Fort Myers. But he quickly decided he would rather be a driver in his dad's branch of the company. It wasn't like he couldn't do the computer stuff, since Frankie is quite intelligent. He just decided he wanted to be out and about rather than being stuck indoors staring at a computer screen all day. The change would surely limit his potential level of earnings at The Bank compared to the pay available for the pressure of crunching numbers, but he was a great deal happier for it.

The funniest part for me is to see Frankie, who is small in height and weight, driving one of the company's big garbage or recycling trucks. The relative size differences just don't fit. And although he is twenty-two, his boyish looks make him appear to be no older than his late teens. Even though Frankie is of age to drink alcohol, he gets his ID checked practically everywhere. Our housemate, Seth, particularly likes to rub in that common occurrence.

From time to time Frankie is also called on to drive the company limousine to and from Page Field or Southwest Florida International Airport to shuttle either company personnel or occasional special visitors. Page Field is home to The Bank's corporate jet. Frankie has seen it, and said it is a Gulfstream G280, which holds up to eight or ten passengers. Being that Frankie is very knowledgeable about the details of most forms of transportation, I believe him when he says that particular model of airplane is a sexy rocket ship. Only the best for The Bank.

As I pulled in the gravel drive of our house on Dinkins Lake Road, I saw Seth's custom van was parked off on a cockeyed angle with its front bumper lodged in a large seagrape bush. Seth is a real character who lives life to the fullest, which includes womanizing and partying on a fairly equal level. It was a safe bet he had rolled back home late, and somewhat inebriated, based on the slipshod parking job. Chances were that a late sleep-in was in progress. When the sun came up on weekends, it was still the middle of the night for Seth.

He is the son of the Food and Beverage Manager at The Bank. At twenty-six, Seth Stanton is the oldest of the three of us living together—and he's quick to bring up that fact. He has been an employee at The Bank longer than Frankie or me. But unlike us, Seth and college didn't mix well, so his attempt at higher education was apparently very brief. And he is certainly the opposite of Frankie in size and stature. Seth is a big and solid athletic guy who looks as though he probably started shaving at around age ten. He has large but handsome facial features, and full, thick hair Hollywood actors would envy.

Seth oversees the processing on incoming shipments of consumable provisions, in addition to keeping tabs on the inventory of all of the stock. He and Frankie interact with each other frequently at work, seeing as Seth manages the receiving of food and beverages at the facility, and Frankie takes away refuse and recyclables. Seth likes to boast about his control of the acquisition of gourmet food and drink. And he is more than willing to point out that Frankie is merely a glorified garbage man.

Frankie takes it in good fun and doesn't let it get to him. I'd have to say that Frankie is about as easy-going as anyone can be. Seth's intermittent barbs glance right off with no effect, making it Frankie's best weapon in reply.

Seth isn't specifically a bully toward Frankie,

though. Seth busts on everybody and anybody whenever possible. He thrives on it indiscriminately to all—except, of course, with the higher ups at The Bank. He knows better. Seth is a real piece of work to deal with as an equal, but he fully understands and respects the power and influence of the hierarchy at The Bank.

I was glad to have not seen either of their fathers, or mine, at the horrible event the night before. Each of our dads held management positions in the company, but none of them were in the ultimate upper crust of the chain of command. Food and beverage, transportation, and building management were all important to the smooth operation of business, but each division consisted of nuts and bolts types of concerns. The *real* power core of The Bank were the ones who were there at the lagoon.

I went into the house and gulped down several large glasses of water before taking one of the longest and most refreshing showers of all time. During the extended washing session, I decided to take it slow on divulging all of the details of the previous night to my housemates. We were all close, and recently we had discussed some enlightening information about the inner workings of The Bank. But now everything had moved into a different realm as far as I was concerned. I felt sure there would come a time in the near future when I'd be compelled to reveal what I had witnessed. A few beers would probably be the catalyst.

For the balance of the weekend I laid low and hung out at the house watching various sports on television, which was an uncommon occurrence for me over the last few years. It was an absent-minded endeavor, though, since I was preoccupied with thinking about the happenings at The Bank. I began my mental review with an experience that had triggered my curiosity several weeks earlier....

4

In the middle of the afternoon on a Thursday, I got a call from my dad. He told me to get one of the maintenance crews together at once for an urgent project. Every project at The Bank was urgent, but this one was painting the office of the President and CEO, Lucien Farr. Dad said Mr. Farr was leaving for the day, so the timing was right to get the painting project completed. To me, it would have made more sense to do the painting on a Friday, so the odor of the fresh paint could dissipate over the weekend. But that is not how things go at The Bank. If the boss wanted something done, it was done when he wanted—no questions asked.

I had met Farr several times, but I couldn't say I really knew him. He was the personification of aloof and impersonal with employees at lower levels. He generally didn't speak to or acknowledge anyone's presence, at least from what I had seen. When Farr walked around The Bank compound, he always kept his head down and avoided eye contact. The only two people I'd ever seen him talk to were his Administrative Assistant, Ava Branstein, and the Security Director, Webb Dunn. They acted as his filters.

When I arrived at Farr's office with the three-man crew, Webb Dunn was waiting in the hallway. I had dealt with him before on quite a few projects, so I knew what to expect. On top of being in charge of the security detail guarding the entire complex, he always seemed to be around to check on anything having to do with the physical plant at The Bank.

To be blunt, Webb Dunn is the most hard-ass bastard I have ever met in my life. Middle-aged, he has a slim but muscular build with a broad and crooked nose, most likely from being broken many years earlier. And his slate-blue eyes can look right through you. Instead of in front, Dunn dresses with his belt buckle off to the side, and he wears his watch so that it reads at an angle on the inner part of his wrist. I assume he doesn't want any wasted motion by having to turn his arm to check the time. Although I have never seen Dunn armed, I would wager he carries a handgun. This is an individual who can strike fear into virtually anyone, especially anyone at The Bank.

Without speaking a word, Dunn put the palm of his hand up to halt the crew, and then motioned for me to follow him into the office. Once inside, he turned and said, "Mr. Farr is gone for the day. I want your crew to paint his office with the standard interior color. Everything in here, as it now sits, is to be returned precisely to its present location. I would recommend taking photos first, to see that the project is completed without a flaw."

"We'll take care of it, sir," I said. "Like it never happened. Right, Mr. Dunn?"

Staring straight at me with a barely noticeable squint of his eyes, he said in a low voice, "Like it never happened."

After Dunn left and the crew started putting drop cloths on the carpeting, I got busy taking pictures with my cell phone of all the horizontal surfaces. I captured shots of the bookcases, credenzas, and tables. In general, everything in the office was neat and organized. But Farr's desk had been left as though he was in the middle of working on something.

The desk wasn't in complete disarray, but there were pens, a pair of reading glasses, and several pads of notes strewn about. Even if we covered it with a drop cloth, I didn't want to take any chances with a serious paint spill getting onto his things. The guys in the crew were very good, but potentially ending up with an unfixable mess was out of the question. I made sure I got several close images of the entire desktop. Since everything was to be returned to its exact position, I considered Farr's desk to be the most important spot.

I decided we should move all of the small stuff in the office to the large table in the conference room that was adjacent through a side door. It was Farr's personal access to the conference room, whose main entry was from the outside hallway. We covered the massive table with a perfectly shaped drop cloth, called a runner, which is designed for use in hallways. As the crew moved loose items from everywhere else in the office, I tackled the job of clearing the top of Farr's desk. I was hoping I had taken enough pictures on my cell phone to ensure every item could be restored to its original place.

When you are twenty-four years old and get instructions from Webb Dunn, it definitely increases your awareness and concern in making certain the work is completed to perfection. If there were any negative follow-up issues with the project, I knew I would be the first person contacted—and that was not a pleasant prospect.

From past experience with these types of jobs, I estimated it would take the three guys on the maintenance crew between two and three hours to paint the office. Since they were very skilled, I thought it best to stay out of the way and let them take care of their business. I still needed to be in the general vicinity until they finished, but I was serving strictly in an advisory capacity. From my standpoint, the most important thing was to make sure everything was returned to the correct location in the office.

Since I had some time, I stepped into the conference room and busied myself by looking over Farr's belongings, which were spread about on the long, rectangular table. I wasn't a spy, but the situation allowed me to take a casual glance at some of the big boss's things. It was more curiosity than anything else.

There was a standard assortment of artwork, table lamps, and books. But it struck me as unusual that there were no personal-type items. No framed college diploma, no family photos, and no awards or certificates with Farr's name on them. In fact, I couldn't find anything with his name at all. There wasn't even hobby or sports memorabilia, or any other outside interest. Everything seemed very sterile. But when thinking about Farr's cold and distant personality, it made sense in an odd way.

I looked over several legal-sized tablets of paper I had moved from his desk earlier. The writing on them was not organized notes or sentences. It was a hodgepodge assortment of indiscernible doodles mixed in with scribbled words and phrases. On both tablets were several pages of what looked to be completely random thoughts and ideas. At least that was the way it seemed to me at first. But the more I studied the pattern of the written words and certain wavy lines between them, the more it seemed as though there was some form of connection or theme. It sure wasn't any formal flow chart, but there did seem to be some type of common link.

The scattering of legible words and letters included *international agenda, quest,* and *fresh global disposition,* followed by the letters *FGD.* On another nearby sheet were *secret oath* and the word *WAIN.* There was scribbling possibly saying, *interest rate manipulation,* and *worldwide control.*

On other pages were random doodles, some of which had no recognizable shape. But there were separate drawings of triangles with a small oval above them. Others were of the sun beaming out toward surrounding stars. I had no idea what it all meant, but it certainly piqued my curiosity.

I pulled out my cell phone and snapped off some close-up pictures of the first few sheets of the note pads, thinking I would like to look them over later in a more relaxed setting. Just as I flipped back to the top sheet of the last tablet for a final photo, the conference room door from the outside hallway burst open. I was so startled I dropped my phone. Into the room stormed Ava Branstein, Farr's closest assistant. I did my best to nonchalantly lean down and pick up my phone from the lavish carpeting.

"Hi, Ms. Branstein," I managed to get out.

Branstein possesses an unfriendly edge and, to be precise, she is hard-as-nails. She is close to being a female version of Webb Dunn—not in appearance but in manner.

"Is everything in order, Bennett?" she asked. I normally go by Ben, but my name is Bennett C. Stradley, III. There were many formalities at The Bank, particularly with the upper command.

"Yes, yes it is," I said. "We moved everything from Mr. Farr's office in here for safety during the painting job. It will all be returned to the same places where things were. Mr. Dunn and I discussed the procedure earlier. The maintenance crew is making good progress. Another couple of hours and we'll be finished."

I blurted all of that out to cover as much information as possible. I was shaking on the inside, and was hoping like mad she hadn't seen what I was doing. I was so glad I had just flipped down the top page on the last tablet so that nothing appeared to have been fiddled with. For all Branstein knew, I could have just been checking messages on my phone. At least that was what I was hoping she thought.

"Mr. Farr," she said, "is having a meeting here in the conference room in the morning. See to it that everything is left in proper order."

"We have it under control, Ms. Branstein," I said.

"Splendid," she said with a squinting stare as she did a turnaround and marched out.

I got a severe case of nervousness after she left. It was one of those experiences where you become more shook up after it is over. Considering it was Ava Branstein, it took me a couple of minutes to calm down. It was a distressing incident.

Several minutes later I took one last rapid-fire picture of the top sheet I had missed, and then stuffed the phone in my pocket. I was tense about the near-catastrophe with Branstein as I walked around without direction until the painting job was finished. There would have been some serious negative consequences getting caught red-handed taking pictures of the boss's notes. For almost two years I'd had a good record of employment at The Bank, so I didn't want to damage it. Yet, I felt okay with what I had done.

When the crew finished the painting job, I helped them place everything back correctly in Farr's office by clicking through and checking the earlier pictures I had taken. I returned everything to the top of his desk. When we were done, I felt confident Farr's entire office was exactly as it had been. Like it never happened, I thought to myself.

An indoor project for a late afternoon in July was a fine assignment to have. During the summer months in Southwest Florida, the outside temperature coupled with the beaming rays of the sun can be very stressful on the body. I have found there are three factors contributing to the level of discomfort. First is whether you are in sunshine or shade—next was if there is a breeze or stillness—and finally if you are being physically active or not. The one extreme is being active in sunshine with little or no breeze. The polar opposite is sitting still in the shade with a nice breeze blowing. Other combinations of the three factors put you somewhere in the middle. The differences are dramatic.

As we were wrapping things up in Farr's office there were some increasingly louder rumbles of thunder thumping in the area. Just as we stepped outside the headquarters building, a fierce rain shower began pouring down. In the summer, it is very common for Mother Nature to dump a large amount of water in a short period of time. The mesh canopy over the complex filters the raindrops some, but when it is really coming down, you can still get soaked in a hurry.

One thoughtful feature in the design of The Bank's complex is the covered walkways between all of the buildings. They serve as a handy awning for either rain or blazing sunshine. It reminded me of the Frank Lloyd Wright-designed house, Fallingwater, in western Pennsylvania. When I was in college at Penn, I took a course on architectural design. Our class made a whirlwind one-day field trip by bus from Philadelphia to the remote location of the famous house. I remember it was a long roundtrip. Fallingwater has the same type of cantilevered coverings over the concrete path from the main residence up to the guest house. And in another similar way with structures designed by Wright, the buildings of The Bank have exteriors blending in with the natural surroundings.

The outside surfaces of all seven buildings in the compound have recycled composite siding in varied shades of tan and green. The roofs of the one-story structures appear flat, but are actually pitched slightly for rain runoff. Having been on all of the roofs, I've seen the splotchy, irregular green coloring of the roofing material. It is apparently yet another security layer in addition to the canopy that camouflages the entire complex from above.

The Frank Lloyd Wright correlation continues with the entrances of each building. The entries and all other exterior doors are very inconspicuous—not grandiose in any way. The parallels go further with the fact that every type of building material utilized is first class in quality. No expense was, or is, spared in any area. Being involved in the management of the facilities, I have to say it is an impressive place to be employed.

5

Since the painting project ran into the early evening, I called my housemate, Frankie, to make a slight alteration to our previous plans. Thursday was the regular night that Frankie, Seth, and I went out for food, beverages, and conversation. And, of course, to survey the female scene. I wanted to let Frankie know I was running late, which was not unusual for any of us due to work-related responsibilities at The Bank. It was generally accepted as the norm.

I told him I'd catch up with them at The Beached Whale over on Fort Myers Beach. We usually rode together unless any of us got hung up at work. We made a practice of picking a bar some-where other than on Sanibel. In addition to the fact that we are younger than most Sanibel residents and visitors, we like to get a little further away to do our socializing. Not only did we want a whole different atmosphere to enjoy some fun, we wanted to avoid issues about where we lived and worked on Sanibel.

More often than not, we divided our outings between Fort Myers and Fort Myers Beach. And they have very different styles. During Spring Break it would be the beach for the college coed exposition. For this night, even though there would be a smaller summer crowd, we wanted to see a good band at The Beached Whale.

As I drove over the Sanibel Causeway to the mainland, the setting sun off to my right blazed a swath of brilliant orange across the Gulf of Mexico and onto the buildings of Fort Myers Beach. I only caught a glimpse of the stunning view, since I had learned back in high school about the dangers of driving while distracted from the task at hand. Some of the films they showed us in Driver's Education scared me in a big way. There were very graphic scenes that have stayed with me ever since. I fully understand a lot of bad things can happen in a hurry if you are doing anything but watching where you are going—with both hands on the steering wheel.

But the problem with being the driver when going over the causeway is that it's easy to get caught up with the panoramic scenery. The Sanibel Lighthouse is at the eastern tip of the island, Pine Island to the north, Fort Myers Beach to the south, the mouth of the Caloosahatchee River meandering around mangrove islands—and nothing but beautiful water in between.

After a few miles, I turned right on San Carlos Boulevard and made my way down to the Matanzas Pass Bridge. For locals, it is commonly known as the Sky Bridge—one of the highest points in Lee County. And what a view. It gives the traveler the mindset, "this is why we came." Straight ahead lies the Gulf of Mexico, and in the distance to the right is the Sanibel Causeway I had gone over a few minutes earlier. Below and to the left in the Pass is the anchorage of a large fleet of shrimp boats. Normally the boats are docked there when it is near a full moon.

Apparently, shrimp are less likely to be netted during that time, so the boats return to port. Laid out beneath in both directions is Fort Myers Beach, the ultimate Americana beach town. It has a little bit of everything a middle-class resort needs: T-shirt shops, beach junk stores, and most importantly, a vast variety of bars and restaurants.

The Beached Whale, where I was headed, is down Estero Boulevard several blocks on the left. It is diagonally across from what is the most iconic establishment on the beach, the Lani Kai Island Resort. The six-story hotel serves as a sea-green beacon when coming over the Sky Bridge. Sitting right on the beach, it is the mecca for Spring Breakers who can practically have the whole structure swaying and gyrating for overlapping weeks at a time. Except for the month or so of various Spring Breaks, the Lani Kai is relatively sedate for the rest of the year. There are, however, occasional exceptions to that general description. It is, after all, the party capital of the island.

As I drove into the parking lot behind The Beached Whale, I negotiated my Jeep through several areas of ponded water. There had been a downpour here also, I thought. I saw Frankie's yellow Camaro a couple of cars down as I pulled into a parking space. As I got out of the air-conditioned interior, I noticed the heavy feel of humidity had lifted. The evening air had become much lighter in the last hour of daylight, and there was a nice breeze.

As I climbed the outside wooden stairway to the upstairs deck, I watched a flock of six or eight pelicans cruise overhead without making a sound. When we went to The Whale, it was our custom to eat up on the deck and people-watch the scene below on Estero Boulevard, before moving downstairs to the inside bar for live music. Frankie and Seth were at a picnic-type table at the front railing of the deck. They had a half-full pitcher of beer in front of them.

"Gentlemen, gentlemen," I said, "what's going on?"

"Not a thing, Bennie," said Seth. "Just waiting on you and having some cold ones. Oh, and Frankie got carded, as usual. Of course, we've been checking out the beach babes wandering around down below. I have to say that the young ladies who come here in the summertime tend to have a slightly rougher edge to them."

"Hey, Ben," said Frankie as I sat down. "So you got hung up with the painting job in Farr's office? Any good stuff in his command post?"

"You bet," I said. After a pause while the waitress delivered a mug for me, I continued, "Some interesting stuff, for sure."

The three of us tried to avoid The Bank as a topic of conversation when we went out, but I was too intrigued by what I had seen on Farr's note pads to not bring it up. When we did talk shop, I was close enough friends with Frankie and Seth to know our exchanges of information would not go any further. I had a strong feeling we all thought the same way on the subject.

"Okay," I said, "I don't know what it means,

but I saw these doodles and notes on pads of paper on Farr's desk, and it has gotten me amped up."

"Ah, Lucien Farr, the Grand Poobah himself," said Seth as he gazed down over the street scene below. "What is going on with our boy, Luke?"

"Well," I said, pulling out my phone and pushing buttons. "I took pictures of what was on the sheets of paper. See what you think."

"Hold on, hold on," said Seth, in an excited tone. "Check this out over there on the sidewalk. That girl is messed up. Look at her, the one with the white shorts stumbling around the lighthouse."

In front of the Beacon Motel, directly across the street, stands a miniature conical lighthouse covered with white seashells. A girl, maybe in her late teens, was staggering around it in circles. She began to yell slurred words we could not make out.

"Oh, man," I said, "I hope she's not by herself."

"No, look," said Frankie, "I think those other kids are with her."

A group of four or five guys and girls of similar age were milling around in the area, but none of them were going over to help the girl who was under the influence in a big way.

"They all look a little too young to be drinking," said Seth. "If the others know her, they don't want to get in trouble by being with her. She is royally shit-faced."

One of the girls in the group was keeping her distance, but even from afar she looked as if she was trying to talk some sense to the drunken one.

"This will not last long," I said. "The cops usually hang out right over there in the 7-11 parking lot."

As the impaired girl's yelling stopped, she leaned her back against the lighthouse and did a slow slide downward until her backside plopped onto the sidewalk. At that point, her friends, or maybe just acquaintances, spread away in a nonchalant fashion in several directions. They wanted no part of the impending situation.

"I think you're right, Seth," said Frankie. "They all look underage."

"Heck, Frankie," said Seth, "then you ought to go on down there. You would fit right in with them as young as you look."

"Oh, boy," I said, "here comes the po-po."

A sheriff's cruiser pulled up halfway onto the sidewalk and its multi-colored lights went on. There was no siren, but the rotating and flashing lights were enough to draw plenty of attention from everyone in the general area. Then a second police car rolled up and its lights went on. At that point, the other young people who apparently were with the inebriated girl were nowhere to be found.

"This may take a while," said Seth. "I bet they all are a bunch of Florida Crackers from inland somewhere like Clewiston. Looks like a standard case of amateurs on summer vacation."

"Okay, Ben," said Frankie, "while the cops are figuring that out, let's see the pictures."

I proceeded to show them the images of the items on Farr's note pads. Seth seemed to have only mild interest. He was much more curious about what was happening across the street. However, I couldn't help but notice Frankie becoming a bit more uneasy with each succeeding picture. When I was finished, I said, "What's up, Frankie? You know anything about this stuff?"

After a moment of hesitation, he said, "Well, I sure don't know everything. But I do know some of what it means. Look, in the beginning when I started working in data processing for a couple of months, I picked up a little about the attempts at interest rate manipulation. It is one of the ways The Bank is trying to make even more money…big money. And the notes about worldwide control are not so far-fetched. That is what they are trying to do."

Changing from what seemed like he was only half-listening, Seth perked right up. "What the hell is with the worldwide control, Frankie? Is that what it has gotten to?"

As Frankie nodded his head several times, I said, "Wait a minute, I know The Bank is involved in international finances, but what is the deal with this?"

"Well," said Frankie, "you know when you hear about some bank getting popped for scamming another bank? If you read the business section in the newspaper, every now and then you see where some big bank got fined."

"You read the business section?" asked Seth.

Frankie gave Seth a sheepish look and said, "Sometimes. What I'm talking about usually has to do with falsifying inter-bank borrowing rates. I have

45

a strong feeling that's what The Bank does on an increasingly bigger scale. They steer rates up or down in order to benefit from the trades they had made. The idea is to profit off of those changing rates. They are doing it with banks—big banks—all over the world. Fixing rates, making trades, borrowing here, lending there and—"

"Screwing them all along the way," said Seth.

"Exactly," said Frankie.

"Yeah," said Seth, "but I didn't know the whole thing had gotten that huge. Nobody tells me anything."

"You know that is the way it works at The Bank, Seth," said Frankie. "Everything is played real close to the vest. Anyway, that is the stuff I picked up on. Nobody in there knows it all, except for a couple of managers at the top of the department. I'm telling you, it is big and probably even bigger yet since I've been out of there."

"Man," I said, "I have been at The Bank practically two years but I didn't know about this."

"I'm ninety-nine percent sure this is what's going on," said Frankie.

"Sounds like highway robbery to me," I said.

"Advanced highway robbery," said Frankie.

"Alright, alright," said Seth, "enough of this crap. Let's get something to eat and then go downstairs for some music. This shoptalk is giving me a headache." Then pointing over the railing, "Yo, dudes, look down there. They are loading the sweet young drunk girl into the cop car."

"I guess she'll be sleeping it off in the pokey

tonight," I said.

"What a humiliating experience," said Frankie.

"No, no," said Seth, "for those harder types, it's a highlighted line item on the partying resume. She'll be famous in her circle of friends."

After we each had a grouper sandwich with fries and slaw—one grilled, one blackened, and one fried, as usual—we went downstairs to the bar. Seth grabbed us a booth close to where the band was setting up. Being a big guy who had a presence in public, Seth was good to have in the group when we were out. He almost always got attention, especially from the ladies. A waitress was right over to the booth to take our order for a pitcher of beer. Seth busted out with a hearty laugh when she carded Frankie.

As for the music, it was somewhat of a reunion of the Biscuit Band. Over the last several years the group had consisted of an ever-changing cast of local musicians, who could always be depended on to play some serious rock and roll. Seth, Frankie, and I had seen them previously on a number of occasions, and we made an effort to catch their show whenever possible. Most of the various members of the band were probably twice our age, or more, but they always would get a room rocking with a tight sound and great vocals, even with varying personnel. They were fun to see and hear.

One of our favorite songs they played was the blues standard, "Call My Job." It has the lines, "Call my job, tell the boss I won't be in, after Friday, Saturday, Sunday, I've had too much weekend."

Considering the aggressive atmosphere at The Bank, we always got a big laugh out of the prospect of bagging work on Monday morning because of too much partying over the weekend. That was never going to happen, for sure. We all saw the irony in it.

During the first set, we worked on a couple of pitchers. Seth did most of the damage on them since he wasn't driving. With the liveliness of the music, the energy level in the bar had certainly increased. Many people were up and dancing. Never one for shyness, especially during a major drinking session, Seth was out of his seat and putting down some steps with several different girls. Because of his size, his rugged good looks, and a contagious smile, finding a dance partner was always easy for Seth. He'd had a few girlfriends since I had known him, but they never lasted very long. He preferred a wider and continuing variety in women. And a willing supply seemed constantly available to him.

After dancing to several songs with one girl, Seth brought her back to our booth while the band took a break. She was attractive and had a nice figure, but as was fairly standard for Seth's taste in women, she had a rather less-than-refined quality about her. Even though he probably could land the best-looking single gal in most establishments, he tended to gravitate toward girls who appeared to possess a somewhat reduced amount of virtue. Seth was lazy that way in the effort department.

As this particular girl sashayed over wearing a clingy sundress, it was apparent that foundation garments were lacking in her attire. Sliding into the booth, Seth said, "Hey guys, this is Angie." Then pointing toward us, "That's Bennie and that's Frankie. And, yes, Frankie is old enough to be in here. He just doesn't look it."

"Hi, Angie," I said, "nice to meet you. What brings you to Fort Myers Beach?"

"Oh," she said, pointing, "I'm with my girlfriends there at that table. We're from Fort Lauderdale. We're over here on vacation this week. How about you guys? You live around here?"

"Yeah," I said, "we live up on Sanibel."

"Whoa, I hear there is money there," she said. "What do you guys do?"

Frankie took over the conversation and gave her the vague, "we work at a research center in a wildlife refuge" line. During some more small talk, Frankie and I caught a few glimpses of Angie's friends at a table across the room. With only a slight shake of our heads, Frankie and I acknowledged that the other girls in the group were not our style. We were each driving home, and it would have taken a good bit more persuasion from the beer to coerce either of us to be motivated to attempt any silly advances toward Angie's friends. It was not in the cards.

Since Frankie was driving them home, Seth had been kicking up the drinking pace for quite a while. The direct result was his manners went flying out the window. He and Angie had been laughing and kidding around, but at one point Seth was inspired to tickle her with a couple of teasing pokes in the ribs. Angie playfully slapped his hand away, but it appeared she wasn't very upset about it.

"I'm going to guess something," said Seth.

"And what would that be?" she said.

"I'll say, besides the sandals you're wearing, you only have two articles of clothing on."

"Well, big boy, then you would be right," said Angie, smiling.

"I don't know what it is," said Seth, "I just have a knack for figuring these kinds of things out. But, seriously, I do have to say you have a great pair of legs."

With a wider, enthusiastic smile, Angie said, "Why, thank you."

"There is only one thing wrong with those legs of yours," he said.

Angie's smile faded as she said, "And what's that?"

"They're not wrapped around my back."

As I whipped my head away to the side, I watched Frankie spew out a mouthful of beer into his mug, which then geysered upward like an erupting volcano. Out of the corner of my eye, I caught the flash of Angie's hand as it delivered a walloping slap to the side of Seth's face. In an instant, Angie popped to her knees and climbed up over him and out of the booth.

There was a pause in conversation during the awkward moment that followed. Frankie was doing his best not to laugh as he grabbed some napkins and mopped up the beer spill on the table. I knew he didn't want to piss Seth off by yukking it up too much, but it was apparent Frankie was having trouble controlling himself. Seth was being his usual confident self, beaming an inebriated grin toward us in an effort to fight off any embarrassment. My mind was churning to come up with something lighthearted to say in an effort to defuse the situation. I tried not to look at Seth's ever-reddening cheek.

Finally I blurted out, "Just another quiet evening on Fort Myers Beach."

"Yeah," said Frankie, fighting back a laugh, "nothing ever happens around here."

Before we knew it, the night manager of The Beached Whale was at our booth. "Everything okay here, gentlemen?" he said with a firm gaze.

"Everything is fine," I said. "We're just going to finish up the rest of this pitcher and head out. No problem."

"I think that would be a good idea," he said.

The check arrived in no time and we proceeded to settle up with our waitress. Frankie and I tried to make a swift and discreet exit of the bar, but not Seth. He strolled out with his head raised in a self-assured demeanor. He wasn't going to let the unfortunate event dampen his spirit. Seth was committed to being himself, regardless of the situation.

When we got to our cars, the muffled thumping sound of the band starting the next set could be heard in the parking lot. As Seth plunked himself down in the passenger seat of Frankie's Camaro, I called over and said I would follow them home. During the drive, I figured Frankie would take the opportunity to release some withheld laughter. I knew he wouldn't overdo it, but at the same time I knew Seth would downplay what had happened as though it was no big deal. Seth's full-size ego on the inside matched his dimensions on the outside.

Coming back over the Sanibel Causeway, a half-moon glistened low over the Gulf of Mexico while countless stars decorated the clear night sky. It was a spectacular view, and I had to remind myself once again to keep my eyes on the road.

I had been watching Frankie's driving from a safe distance on the way home. He was steady as she goes, as usual. I knew Frankie would be fine, since we both had been fairly modest with the drinking once we went downstairs to see the band. The manager encouraging us to leave provided additional assistance in that regard.

When I came onto Sanibel and turned up Periwinkle Drive, my mind drifted back to the issue of Farr's notes and what they meant. Frankie and Seth had enlightened me to a point, but they had also served to pique my curiosity further. I got the impression both of them were content to write it all off to "business as usual" at The Bank. But that wasn't the way I was starting to feel. I was interested in finding out more.

6

A week or so later I was sent to supervise a crew assigned to replace carpeting in the Data Processing Department. I had been mulling over the various issues concerning The Bank, but I hadn't had any projects in or near the D/P offices. I figured this might be a chance to nose around a little in the nerve center of the company. I was prepared to be as careful as possible. I didn't even know what I would be looking for, and I certainly didn't have access to any of the computers and their secure systems anyway. But at least I would be at the heart of where things happened.

I reported to the data center late in the day with a two-man crew. Work would be winding down, so the idea was to get the job completed with minimal disruption of normal daily activity.

There had been a coffee spill, which made a sizeable stain on the carpeting in an open area of the large computer room. I saw the brownish mark was clearly visible, but it seemed to me a thorough shampooing would have taken it out. That thinking, however, was not the way The Bank operated. Instead of making a repair of virtually any type, the standard company policy was to always replace what was flawed with new material. As previously mentioned, money is never an object in such cases. Make it perfect and do it now, period.

The fortunate part of the project was very little furniture needed to be moved. Besides, there was no chance the crew would be permitted to move any of the computers, even if I gave them a hand. The two maintenance guys were not just going to cut out the stained spot. They had been previously instructed to replace the entire open area, which bordered walls and doorways on three sides. On the fourth side they would feather the new side into an existing edge. I had worked with the same two men before, and knew they would do a faultless job.

As they got under way, I looked across the computer room where only a handful of employees remained. I took immediate notice of Gwen Copeland. We had exchanged small talk a couple of times in the company café. Gwen had only been with The Bank for five or six months. Her uncle was Harris Copeland who headed the entire information and data section of the company. He was Gwen's legacy connection at The Bank. Aside from that, and more importantly to me, she is very pretty. Gwen is a little above average in height, with a slender figure and long brunette hair. And her bright blue eyes are really something. Having only talked to her for a short time on previous occasions, I could tell she was sharp. She had a wonderful combination of brains and good looks.

As Gwen was buttoning things up at her desk, and also when she was starting to walk toward one of the side exits, I could sense a certain negative gloom about her. It was a look I hadn't seen before. She hadn't noticed me so, in a casual way, I strategically scooted over to intercept her path.

"Hi, Gwen," I said, "how's it going?"

"Oh, hi there, Ben," she said, "I didn't see you here. Guess I was thinking about something else. Well, it's going. That's about it."

"Well, uh, I'm in here to supervise the guys doing the carpet replacement," I said. "They'll be at it for a while. How about if I walk out with you?"

"That would be fine," she said. "I'm just not quite with it today. Sorry."

As we left the building I could tell for sure something was bothering Gwen. I had only gotten some one-syllable responses from her to a couple of trivial questions I asked. I have never been much for prying into other people's business, but I was thinking this might be an opportunity to make some inroads with her. As we got to her car, a dark, charcoal gray sky made it look as though we were in for yet another late-afternoon thunderstorm. I figured I better make my pitch in a hurry.

"Looks like we may get bombed with rain again today," I said.

"Yeah," she said with a disinterested tone to her voice, "nothing new for the summer around here."

"So, Gwen," I said, "I don't mean to be abrupt or anything, but would you want to meet me for a drink later on? You know, just talk. I could meet you at the Sanibel Grill. It's right next to The Timbers Restaurant on Tarpon Bay Road. It's a sports bar. Say around nine?"

"Yes, I know where you mean. I've been to The Timbers for dinner a few times. Well, that sounds good to me," she said, her face brightening a little. "And I could use a little casual conversation. See you at nine."

Just as she turned to get into her car, rain started pouring down in buckets. We exchanged waves as I sprinted to get under the outside walkway overhang. Getting soaked by a rainstorm is nothing unusual during the Southwest Florida summer. But I hardly noticed I was drenched until I got back inside the air-conditioned building. Even then, I was concentrating far more on Gwen, and our get-together, which was only a matter of hours away. Any undercover investigative work I had been considering while in the Data Processing office was shifted to the back burner. I was enthusiastically looking forward to being with her.

It was a good idea I had suggested meeting Gwen at the Sanibel Grill instead of arranging to pick her up. Our date was spontaneous, so I thought it was best to keep everything informal. Plus, I knew from our earlier conversations she lived with her aunt and uncle in The Sanctuary. That quaint little neighborhood is a collection of some major upscale homes, surrounded by a pristine golf course that traverses the roads by way of golf cart crossings. My parents lived there, too. In addition, most of the higher-ups at The Bank lived in a close cluster in The Sanctuary. Lucien Farr wanted his top lieutenants nearby in case he decided to call a meeting in the middle of the night, which I heard happened upon occasion.

Those homes were not far at all from the much more modest house the guys and I rented on Dinkins Lake Road. But I knew it was a bad idea to be seen going in or out of any residence in The Sanctuary except my parents' place. With the way politics functioned at The Bank, there was no sense planting the seed of a gossip topic—especially in the middle of the bigwig neighborhood. Meeting Gwen at the Sanibel Grill was the best strategy.

Nine o'clock could not come fast enough. After the crew finished up the carpet repair project, to perfection I might add, I blasted home for a sandwich and a shower. It was my second shower of the day, but I wanted to be as fresh as possible for the upcoming encounter.

I was pretty giddy about seeing Gwen outside the work environment. Interaction at The Bank was stilted enough as it was. The chats we'd had at work had just been courteous exchanges of general information. And our conversations had always been nearby other employees. I was looking forward to talking with Gwen in a more relaxed atmosphere where we could be more ourselves, and get to know each other.

The Timbers, which is right next door to the Sanibel Grill, is a very nice restaurant that was frequently patronized by the upper-echelon at The Bank. But since it was a weeknight, and we weren't meeting until nine, I felt fairly confident we wouldn't be seen by anyone who knew either of us.

I got to the parking lot about eight-thirty since I wanted to be sure to arrive before Gwen.

I thought it was the polite thing to do, plus, I was too anxious to stay home any longer. Since it was early August, there was still some fading daylight, which turned out to be fortunate. As I was about to get out of my Jeep, I saw Webb Dunn and his wife walk out of The Timbers Restaurant and then pass right behind me. I stayed put with my head turned away until they drove off. Dunn was the one person I wanted to have the least contact with as possible. He was the prototype of a stern disciplinarian who was endowed with unrestricted authority. A scary man.

After the coast was clear, I went inside the Sanibel Grill. I took a stool at the bar where Gwen could see me when she came in. It wasn't very crowded, which would be normal for a weeknight in the summer. I ordered a draft beer and surveyed the televisions that were showing multiple baseball games. On the screen directly in front of me was the Phillies game.

Growing up on the Main Line just west of Philadelphia, I had been a Phillies fan since I was a kid. But during the last few years while I worked at The Bank, I had gravitated away from closely following baseball, or most any other sport. The Bank had a way of consuming you. It was a tunnel-vision focus on work that was drummed into you, whether said or simply implied. The Phillies were playing their archrivals, the New York Mets. I got so absorbed in the game, I didn't even notice Gwen enter and take a stool next to me.

"Hey there, stranger," she said. "You come here often?"

Startled, I turned and said, "Oh, hi, Gwen. I guess I was getting too caught up in the baseball game. It's the Phillies against the hated Mets."

"Really? The hated Mets is it? I happen to have grown up on Long Island, and have always been a Mets fan."

"Uh-oh," I said, smiling. "Looks like I got this little social gathering off to a rousing start. Sorry. Maybe we ought to talk about something besides baseball."

"The baseball is no big deal," she said. "With the way things have been going lately, I'd just as soon talk about baseball, or the weather, or anything, I guess."

After Gwen ordered a glass of wine, we toasted our glasses in a peace offering. I was curious about what was bothering her, but I thought the best thing to do was ease into it slowly. After all, this was an unofficial first date.

"So, you grew up on Long Island," I said. "What part?"

"Glen Cove," she said. "It's on the North Shore."

"I've been right near there," I said. "I had a friend at the University of Pennsylvania who came from Sea Cliff. I went up there with him one time to his parents' house."

"Yes," said Gwen, "Sea Cliff is the next town over. You went to Penn? So you're an Ivy Leaguer."

"Indeed I am," I said. "How about you?"

"I went to Skidmore," she said. "It's in upstate New York."

"In Saratoga Springs, isn't it?" I was duly impressed with her Alma Mater. Skidmore College is a very exclusive private school. During our exchange, I became conscious of the fact that I couldn't take my eyes off of her. I was becoming very attracted to Gwen.

"Yes it is," she said. "While I was going to college I used to go up before the start of the fall semester and work the month of August at the Saratoga Race Course. That is the only time they have live horse racing at the track. The meeting runs into the first week of September and ends at Labor Day. It's roughly a six-week extravaganza. And it was nice to earn some spending money right before school started."

"That is neat," I said. "What did you do?"

"I was a hostess in the Club House. Basically I was looking after the money crowd, and their various wants and needs. But I did enjoy it. It was a different type of education than going to college. I'm glad I experienced it. I got some real-life culture, and made a few bucks along the way."

"I've never been up to Saratoga."

"You would love the track," she said. "The whole place is so cool. It is the oldest sporting venue of any kind in the United States. It first opened during the Civil War, if you can believe that. And the Horse Racing Hall of Fame is just down the street."

In the midst of what was a nice give-and-take conversation, I noticed a wave of gloomy change come over Gwen's face. It visibly altered her like the flip of a switch, and it seemed to catch her off guard.

All of a sudden she wasn't there.

"Look, Gwen," I said, "I am sure it's none of my business, but are you all right?"

"Oh, I'm sorry," she said, snapping out of her funk a bit. "It's just that there are some things starting to happen at work. Some serious things. I'll be okay. I really shouldn't talk about it. I thought coming out tonight to meet you would help take my mind off work."

"Well," I said, smiling, "we could always talk about the baseball game."

She smiled, put her hand on the top of my forearm with a gentle grip, and said, "Maybe for tonight, it might be a good idea."

We had a couple more drinks and chit-chatted on lighter topics. My feelings for Gwen were sky-rocketing, but I held back from pursuing whatever issues she was dealing with. I was trying to control myself from coming on too strong, which was not my style with girls anyway. But I was feeling an extraordinary attraction to Gwen, so it created a more difficult undertaking to remain reserved. I wanted to help her in some way if I could.

Around eleven we decided to call it a night. People our age have always been well-known for not even going out on a Thursday night until ten or later, and staying out until all hours on a so-called school night. But if you worked at The Bank that reckless behavior was not a good idea. Promptness, perfection, and strict attention to detail with a clear head trumped anything and everything else. Essentially, The Bank was your life.

I paid our tab and we walked out to Gwen's car. We both turned toward each other and simultaneously started, "I'd like to see you…" With that, we embraced in a full bear hug. Although she wasn't trembling I could sense a troubled clinging from her. Gwen pulled her head back while we were still holding each other tight and it evolved into a warm, affectionate kiss. However long the kiss lasted, it wasn't long enough for me, and I was hoping the same was true for her.

We exchanged cell phone numbers and made plans to get together on the upcoming Saturday night. There was no mistaking a certain chemistry existed between us. Although, I was beginning to feel somewhat torn between my newborn infatuation with Gwen, and the knowledge that some form of dilemma was brewing in her life at The Bank. Even though I was eager for things to progress between us, I decided I should proceed with controlled caution until whatever issues she was dealing with came more to light. Considering the intense atmosphere at The Bank under normal conditions, voluntarily adding more drama was not a good idea. But the excitement our kiss had created in me was winning the battle over prudence.

7

Gwen and I had discussed the matter of her living with her aunt and uncle. Although she lived in a suite with a separate entrance on a wing of the large house, we agreed the tactful course of action was for me not to be seen coming over to pick her up. Just like me, she was a responsible young adult who could make her own decisions—but our shared concern was the uncomfortable situation we would be creating in regard to our employment at The Bank. We thought the sensible thing to do was to drive in separate cars for our date.

We decided to meet on Saturday evening at six at the Olde Sanibel Shoppes where Periwinkle intersects Tarpon Bay Road. It is a small shopping plaza that features two of my favorite businesses on Sanibel. The Over Easy Café is a great breakfast and lunch spot. I'd had many tasty meals on their covered outdoor patio. Right next door is Suncatchers' Dream, a classy and unique gift shop. When a nice present was needed, I always felt confident in finding something special and distinctive there. It was my go-to store for gifts for my mother at Christmas and her birthday.

The plaza and its parking areas are surrounded by trees and shrubbery, which made it a good out-of-sight spot to leave Gwen's car. And, all of the businesses would be closed before six. We wanted to assure our secrecy from any people who worked at The Bank. Gwen and I felt the same way about the need for taking extra precautions.

I got to the Shoppes fifteen or twenty minutes early and parked my Jeep off to the right where the lot is more secluded. I thought about Gwen with tremendous anticipation the whole time I was waiting. Promptly at six, Gwen wheeled her Audi sedan into the parking space next to me.

"Hey there," by both of us as we got out. Gwen came right up to me and we exchanged a brief kiss. It was much lighter than a few nights earlier, but it got the evening off to a good start.

As we got into the Jeep, I said, "I know a place off of Sanibel where we can go for dinner. It's called Fresh Catch Bistro over on Fort Myers Beach."

"That sounds fine to me," said Gwen. "Let's get away."

I was trying to judge Gwen's mood in terms of her stress level. And my thinking was, so far, so good. I got the impression she would have ridden with me over to Miami for dinner if that was what I had in mind.

Fresh Catch Bistro is located roughly at the midpoint of Fort Myers Beach. It sits on the sand overlooking the Gulf of Mexico. At other times of the year, I would have suggested we sit on the outdoor deck, but since it was summer, the air-conditioned dining room was the obvious choice. Since it was the off-season, we didn't need a reservation and there wasn't a long wait. We were promptly seated at a window overlooking the beach and the Gulf.

"Nice view, huh?" I said.

"Sure is," she said. "I've only been over here on Fort Myers Beach a couple of times. It has more of a beach town feel than Sanibel."

"Yeah," I said, "it's a different atmosphere in many ways. It fits the definition of a beach town perfectly. Where we live on Sanibel is more of an isolated environment that definitely doesn't fall under the category of mainstream America."

We had cocktails while we looked over the menu. Gwen ordered grilled grouper, and I chose the seared tuna steak. Ordinarily I would have gotten the tuna blackened or Caribbean jerk style, but I didn't want to take any chances of having unpleasant breath. I even changed from the Pan Asian topping to tropical fruit salsa to match what Gwen had ordered, for the same reason. I was thinking ahead.

During a delicious dinner, our conversation centered on light and ordinary generic topics. But after the waiter cleared the table and we sat back with our glasses of wine, Gwen appeared more serious and said, "The issues at The Bank that I was anxious about the other night haven't gone away. And probably won't."

She turned and looked out at the beautiful view for a minute. I could tell she was struggling with divulging confidential information, as it was absolutely forbidden at The Bank. And it was easy for me to see that Gwen knew she was wandering into dangerous territory. I decided not to press her. It was her option to open up if she wanted. But I was sensing a trust developing between us and, on all other subjects, it seemed as though we were clicking together.

She turned back and said, "I'm not sure what you know about how The Bank operates."

"Well," I said, "I've talked a little bit about it with my housemates. Frankie, who is one of them, worked for a while in Data Processing, like you. But he switched to being a driver in his dad's department before you started. He let me in on some of the finagling that goes on."

I wanted Gwen to think I knew more than I really did, just to see what she would tell me. If it was going to make her feel better to get something off her chest, I was an eager listener. I was already curious for more details about The Bank's methods, ever since Frankie and Seth talked about it the night we were at the Beached Whale. But, with Gwen, I made the conscious decision to skip the subject of the pictures I had taken in Farr's office. I could always show her later. I sure didn't want Gwen to think I was some kind of a snoop.

"The Bank," she said, "is becoming a world leader in ripping off other financial institutions. Because they have such vast monetary resources, in general, they leverage their strength to gain an advantage. The little old business we work for on Sanibel goes toe-to-toe with some of the largest banks in the world, and usually comes out ahead."

I was dying to ask her for more details, including how The Bank acquired its money, but I figured that was going a bit too far. I didn't want to come off as trying to take advantage of Gwen's knowledge, but I was certainly becoming more and more inquisitive.

"Yeah," I said, "I know The Bank has its ways."

"Do you know about the LIBOR?" asked Gwen.

"I've heard the term, but not specifically."

"It stands for London inter-bank offered rate," she said. "It is sort of a daily bidding system in London between the major world banks. Our bank has several representatives stationed over there who carry out the process. They manipulate information that is used to set a critical interest rate. Then they try to maneuver rates either up or down. Most of the time it works out to the good. But it's a highly illegal way to operate."

"Frankie also told me about how other big banks are popped from time to time for that same kind of practice."

"Well," she said, "our employer happens to be expert at it...and ruthless at it. Somehow they manage to fly under the radar of the financial regulatory system in comparison to the scrutiny other large world banks get. The Bank does the nice-guy thing where they help other big banks, and then suck them in with a you-help-me-back plan. I think there is an ulterior motive in everything they do. There is this incessant drive to come out on top financially."

Gwen bowed her head a touch and then turned and looked out over the Gulf. No doubt, the cocktail before dinner, followed by several glasses of wine, had helped her open up. And she was realizing it. On the bright side, I didn't think she would have said the things she did if she didn't trust me. It made me attracted to her even more. I decided it was a good time for a change of subject and venue.

"There is a movie theater," I said, "just a little down the road from here. The shows start at nine, so we could make it if we leave now."

"That sounds great," she said, looking relieved.

I took care of our check and we walked outside. The sun was setting and it blazed a beautiful scene across the Gulf. From high-altitude clouds down to the surface of the water, a brilliant spectrum of reds, oranges, and dark blues splashed across Mother Nature's canvas. It was stunning. After Gwen and I had walked only a short distance onto the beach, we turned on dual impulse, embraced and kissed. The exchange of affection was as intense and exciting as the earlier evening we had been together.

We drove down to the Beach Theater but never made it inside. An extended make-out session in the parking lot had overruled. Eventually, I suggested we head back to more familiar territory. On the drive back to Sanibel, my Jeep was riding on air.

When we got to Gwen's car, the parking lot was empty, dark, and quiet. I pulled past Gwen's Audi to an even more remote spot. Without delay, the hugging and kissing started up again. Time slipped away and our emotions intensified. Gwen pulled back a bit and put her index finger on my lips. With a sweet smile she whispered, "Not tonight. Let's spend some extended time together next weekend. You know, get away."

"And maybe never come back?" I said. "Just kidding. I think that would be a really good idea. But next weekend seems like a long time from now."

"We can make it," she said. "Let's be careful and take it a step at a time. We both have a lot riding on our jobs at The Bank."

"Yeah, I guess we do. Next weekend it is. I'll come up with a plan."

"I bet you will," she said, laughing.

We walked to her car and engaged in a lengthy goodbye. After we finally tore ourselves away from each other, I followed her back up SanCap Road to Wildlife Drive, and then a left on Wulfert. When I turned onto Dinkins Lake, I knew she only had a few hundred yards to go until she got to Baltusrol Court and her uncle's house. Whatever I did when I got home was a forgettable blur of nothingness. All I could think about was Gwen.

8

The next six days were the longest and slowest of my life. But I plodded through as best I could. During the day, I forced myself to focus on projects

I was assigned to handle at work. Talking to Gwen at The Bank was not an easily manageable process, and it would only raise interest and suspicion among our co-workers anyway. I did talk to her on the phone several evenings during the week. The other nights were nondescript and boring. On Thursday night, I went out with Frankie and Seth up to the City of Fort Myers. We hit several clubs, but the entertainment and the girls were irrelevant to me. Overall, it was a lackluster night. I was too preoccupied and giddy in anticipation of spending the weekend with Gwen. I told the guys I was getting away for the weekend, but skipped the part about Gwen. Even with my housemates, I didn't feel like I had reached the point of bringing it up. I decided to leave well-enough alone.

Friday crawled along at a snail's pace. During the afternoon, I was sent to supervise a crew doing repair work on the siding and roof of the main administration building. There had been a water leak in the upper corner of the entry foyer. The summer rains on Sanibel are forceful enough to find the tiniest of openings. The fact that the problem was in the foyer area might make it seem not so critical compared to drips of water onto a computer, but at The Bank everything is critical.

The job was finished before five, complete with priming and painting of the interior ceiling and wall. I was fortunate to be able to make a timely getaway from work. A job running late was always an uncertainty with afternoon projects.

Climbing up on the roof several times had

left me soaked in sweat, which necessitated some freshening. I drove home and, before I took a quick shower, loaded the Jeep with a small cooler filled with sodas and bottled water. In a larger cooler I packed a dozen beers and a bottle of wine. Since it was summer, one duffle bag was plenty for my clothes. I had packed it several nights earlier with a couple pairs of shorts, several nice tee shirts, and a bathing suit.

While I was drying off from the shower, I checked my phone and listened to a message from Gwen. She, too, had gotten a break and left work on time. And, she would meet me at the same parking lot in the Olde Sanibel Shoppes at six-thirty. What bothered me, though, was the disturbed sound of her voice on the message. It certainly came off as though she was still bothered by something. It made me feel uneasy.

I pulled into the shopping plaza at twenty after six and Gwen was already there. As I parked next to her and looked over, she was staring straight ahead with a look of dejection. When she realized I was standing next to her car, she snapped out of whatever was on her mind and smiled as she got out. Before I could say anything, she grabbed me and planted a hard kiss on my lips.

When it ended, I said, "Is everything okay?"

"Yes," she said, "everything is fine. Let's get going to wherever you want to go. I'm ready."

I grabbed her bag and tossed it in as we jumped into the Jeep and got on our way. I knew there was something eating at her, but she was doing a good job of masking it. I decided to follow her cue.

"Gwen," I said, "I wanted to cut down on travel time so I thought we ought to go back over to Fort Myers Beach for the weekend. Even though it's not far, I'd say the chances of running into any Sanibel people are about nil. Like we said last Saturday at dinner over there, the two places are close in miles but light years apart in their clientele. This way we can maximize the time we have. "

"Look, Ben," she said with a smile, "I don't care where we go. It's fine with me. Just being together and away from here is going to be great."

"I think it will be fun," I said. "I booked us a cottage at a place called the Silver Sands Villas. We passed it last Saturday night. It's at the upper end of the island near The Beached Whale where my housemates and I go sometimes. I checked the place out and it is clean and neat. They even received some kind of white glove award. There are only twenty-two units and it's on a canal. Plus, we can walk everywhere we want to go. The beach is right across the street."

"Cannot wait," she said.

During the half-hour drive, Gwen was quiet except for responding to things I brought up. I felt sure she was preoccupied with a problem. But I was really hoping we could have a good weekend.

We got to the Silver Sands and checked in to a perfectly spotless room. Both inside and out, the lodging had a Key West style and feel to it. Since we both had packed lightly, I only had to make two trips to the Jeep to bring our belongings inside while Gwen started setting things up in the room.

Just as I closed the door and set down the two coolers, Gwen turned away from the sparkling vanity area and embraced me with a firm squeeze. After swaying together with her head on my shoulder for only a moment, we collapsed onto the bed. There was a desperate urgency in Gwen's passion, and I was compelled to match her emotion, heartbeat for heartbeat. It was thrilling…

Around nine, we walked across Estero Boulevard to the Gulfshore Grill. It was just after sunset. I had heard the restaurant was housed in the oldest building on Fort Myers Beach, and that its food was first-rate. Seated at a table next to the windows, we had a perfect view of the nearby pier slowly slipping into the darkness. We shared a bottle of wine and enjoyed an excellent seafood dinner.

I'd had a girlfriend in college, but we had parted ways after graduation. The way I was now feeling about Gwen went far beyond earlier romances. This was turning into my first serious adult relationship with a woman. And it was a good feeling.

As on our previous date, Gwen waited until we had finished eating before bringing up what must have been on her mind all along.

"Things have gone from bad to worse at work," she said. "I didn't tell you this last weekend when we went out to dinner, but I knew then some form of breach in the security of the data system has been happening recently. There has been this constant undercurrent of stress and tension in the whole department. It's been as if everyone is always looking around wondering who is responsible. No one seems to trust anyone else. It's not spoken, but the anxiety is there."

"So what is your take?" I said. "Any idea who might be the guilty party?"

Gwen turned and gazed out the window at the fleeting colorful glimmers in the sky. For a moment, she got a faraway look in her eye. On her cheek facing toward me, I saw a thin stream of tears run down her face. Gwen caught herself and did a brief, drying dab with her napkin. After she was composed, Gwen looked straight at me and with firm confidence said, "It's my uncle."

"What?" I said. "Your uncle is the head of Data Processing. Why would he intentionally harm the security?"

"Look, Ben," she said, "I don't know how to soft-pedal this. To begin with, Uncle Harris is an alcoholic, or at least he is a tremendous drunk. One night early this week, I wasn't sleepy so I decided to do a load of clothes. I went out of my bedroom, which is in a wing off of the main part of the house, and walked down the hallway to the laundry. I heard the angry muttering of my uncle's voice coming from the living room. I don't eavesdrop on my aunt and uncle, but I could not help but overhear. He had to be alone, and was talking to himself with very slurred, drunken speech. What I could make out was this heated rant with lines like, 'I've got to get rid of him' and 'That bastard, Morrison, is going down.'"

"That's Tyler Morrison?" I said. "He's number two in your department, directly under your uncle."

"Right. Then he said something like, 'Gotta do some damage to his files.' And then, 'That bastard is not getting my job.' Then on the way back from the laundry room—and I was trying to be very quiet—his words were so garbled I couldn't understand anything. Just as I was almost to my room, there was the loud crashing sound of a glass breaking on the tile floor. I scooted into my room, closed the door, and didn't go back to hang up my load of clothes until early the next morning. I don't know what to do, Ben. This is awful. It's really scaring me."

"I've talked to Tyler a few times," I said. "He seems to be a good guy. What's with the animosity? It sounds like your uncle is paranoid about him."

"Well," she said, "first off, Tyler Morrison *is* a good guy, and he is also very smart and very ambitious. I think he is determined to keep moving up at The Bank. The bad part is I think my uncle sees that determination in him, and fears him. I have this sneaking suspicion Uncle Harris has gotten to where he is at The Bank by stepping on people around him. I think with his drinking he also realizes he is not the sharp-minded whiz he once was. Especially compared to Tyler. I'm sure he sees him as dangerous competition."

"Wow," I said. "So what's with the part of it about damaging Morrison's files?"

"It would be easy to do," Gwen said. "I would bet that is exactly what Uncle Harris has already done to undermine the secure systems we have. It's what has everyone walking on eggs. He can gain access to everything, including everyone's files and records. At nights or on weekends or whenever Tyler is out of the office, my uncle could be sabotaging his computer. And it sounds like he is planning on stepping up that course of action."

"What a mess," I said. "I don't know what to tell you. I sure don't want to see you get involved in this, though."

"Well, I think my uncle has a very specific target. I'm not worried for me. I'd just hate to see Tyler get fired...or worse. He has a wife and two young kids."

Just as I was getting ready to speak, Gwen started again. "Ben, there's something else. And I'm not sure what it means. But last night when my aunt and uncle went out to dinner, I went into his home office. I don't do that sort of thing, Ben, but this whole subject has been bothering me so much I had to do something. On his desk was a plainly written note. It said, 'Friday night, 8/12 – 9:00pm – Morrison – Gator Lagoon – WAIN.' It was so specific, I memorized it."

"That's next Friday," I said. It struck me that, just like me in Farr's office, Gwen had taken an action not in her nature by looking around where she probably shouldn't have.

"Yes, it is next Friday," she said. "Do you know what the Gator Lagoon is?"

"No," I said. "I guess it's somewhere in Ding Darling. I know that a little way back on Wildlife Drive from the entrance lane to The Bank, there are several gator observation decks for visitors to the refuge. But I've never heard of anything called a Gator Lagoon, though."

"Ben," she said, "I'm going up to Long Island next weekend for my cousin's wedding. And I have been thinking about asking you to go with me, but at this point I don't think it would be a good idea. I'll let you know if I find out anything else during the week. But I don't want you getting involved in any of this either. It just doesn't sound good."

"Gwen," I said, grasping her hand, "first, I think you are right about going to the wedding on your own. And second, I'm not planning on getting involved. Let's just try to put all of this on the back burner and enjoy our weekend together." She smiled and bowed her head. Then after a pause I said, "I think you are something."

Tightening her hand on mine and looking up at me, she said, "I think you are something, too."

We left the Gulfshore and walked on the beach for a while. We were bathed by a warm summer breeze, and the clear night sky sparkled with a million stars. As we headed back to our room, I decided I would show Gwen the pictures on my phone from Farr's office. But it would have to wait until the next day. We had tabled our discussion of issues at The Bank, and I had no intention of spoiling the rest of the night by bringing it up again.

We freshened and made preparations for bed. What followed was a delightful night of love-making. We became as one. It was as if neither of us wanted the excitement to end by going to sleep. We both continued to be energized by our youthful stamina. In Gwen's case, it was as if she was setting free the pent-up emotions she had been suppressing.

And with the spirited infatuation I was feeling toward Gwen, I was a willing partner. We could not get enough of each other. Slumber finally overcame us, and in the blink of an eye it was morning.

During the balance of our weekend getaway we savored every moment together. I did show Gwen the pictures of Farr's notes and doodles. We both noticed the reference of WAIN, but it meant nothing to either of us. Her understanding of what the other writings meant was limited, but she felt sure, at the core of it, there was some form of fraternal bond among the power elite at The Bank. The more we tried to piece together how it was all related, the more distressed we became with The Bank and the way it operated. We did our best to limit the shoptalk and concentrate on each other.

Without a doubt, it was the most enjoyable weekend of my life, and it was evident Gwen was feeling the same way. Including the first two dates, our overall time together had been brief. But by the end of the weekend, we had reached the point where we were crazy about each other.

9

During the following week, Gwen and I met at the Sanibel Grill later in the evening on two nights, including Thursday. Since it was the night before she was flying up to New York for her cousin's wedding, we had to be together. The other evenings we engaged in extended phone conversations. Both of us continued to agree on maintaining an air of secrecy about our association. It was the best plan in the short term.

Over the course of the days before she left, I methodically mounted my resolve to seek out whatever occurrence was to take place on Friday night regarding Tyler Morrison. I didn't breathe a word of my plan to Gwen. It was a sure thing she would offer strong discouragement for me to set myself up for any potentially dangerous situation. However, because I am a Taurus, I pressed on with my bullish determination to investigate the impending occasion.

As detailed earlier, the following night at the Gator Lagoon, and thereafter, was eventful. Like none I had ever experienced. It had changed me and had emboldened my increasing distaste for The Bank. I quietly rode out the rest of that weekend. My best ally in the fight to avoid reflecting on the horrible happening was to concentrate on thinking about Gwen. Between having been an eyewitness to the demise of Tyler Morrison, and my skyrocketing fervor for Gwen, my life had become far more complicated in a short period of time.

Gwen flew back on Monday and we went out in the evening. I could not bring myself to tell her about what had happened. Overall, I knew it would throw her mood into a downward spiral, especially regarding her uncle's presence in the group. Plus, I knew she would be traumatized by my risky involvement. I kept steering the conversation toward her weekend at the wedding. She had not yet returned to work, so she did not know of Tyler Morrison's departure from the office.

When we were together again on Wednesday night, I continued to hold my tongue on the subject— even when Gwen brought up the several-day absence of Tyler at work. "No one in the department has said anything at all," she said. "Everybody has been keeping their head down and concerning themselves with the business of The Bank. This is really worrying me, Ben. I hope everything is okay."

I swallowed hard and offered something bland, like, "I'm sure some information will come out." I had been struggling with what happened. I didn't want to tell Gwen what I had witnessed before I thought through the potential consequences. I had already decided to tell Frankie and Seth when we went on our usual Thursday night outing. I figured it would be a dress rehearsal for my future explanation to Gwen.

Thursday after work we rolled out in Seth's van and headed toward Fort Myers. When it was all three of us, we usually took the van so we wouldn't be cramped in Frankie's Camaro or my Jeep. Seth also liked the spaciousness of the van, especially if he could be fortunate enough to coerce a girl to join him in it for a while. Typically, Frankie would do the driving on the return trip since Seth would practically always have had the most to drink. I felt more comfortable with Frankie at the wheel anyway. Even when he wasn't drinking, Seth tended to get into boisterous conversation and look at everything *but* the road. Frankie, on the other hand, took driving very seriously. He was, after all, a pro.

As we were cresting the tall bridge of the Sanibel Causeway on the way to the mainland, Frankie noted, "That point at the base of the bridge where the boat ramps are is called Punta Rassa. Many years ago it was a staging area for cattle to board boats for shipment either up north or to Cuba. In many cases, they herded the cattle from far inland."

"Is there anything you don't know, Frankie?" said Seth.

"Yes, there is," said Frankie, "but I'm working on learning about those things one by one."

I always got a kick out of the friendly banter between those two guys. It was a good distraction to take my mind off of my forthcoming disclosure.

We headed up the royal palm tree-lined McGregor Boulevard toward The Edison. It is a restaurant and bar on the grounds of the Fort Myers Country Club. The Edison is a hopping nightspot where young adults gather for drinks and socializing.

I was contemplating how and when I would get into the story with the guys. I suggested we stop and get something to eat at the McGregor Café, which is located just south of The Edison. I figured it would be a more low-key environment to talk than the hubbub of the club scene. We had eaten on the outside patio at the Café once before, but since it was August we opted for the inside air-conditioning. As poor luck would have it, there were patrons at almost every table, including the two booths adjoining ours. I didn't want to have anyone overhear what I was going to say. Plus, I didn't know how Seth and Frankie would react to the story, so I waited until we were finished and were walking to the van.

Before we got in, I said, "Look, guys, I've got some very bad news about something I saw last Friday night."

"Let me guess," said Seth, "you caught Farr and his pit bull assistant, Ava Branstein, making out?"

"Look, Seth," I said, "this is serious shit."

"Okay, okay," he said, laughing, "go ahead."

"I caught wind that some kind of event was going to happen regarding an issue that had been festering in the Data Processing Department. I had heard it was going to take place at the Gator Lagoon that night, but I didn't know exactly where that was."

"Is it near the Alligator Viewing Platforms?" asked Frankie.

"I was thinking the same thing," I said, "and it's not too far from them. I inched on foot through the mangroves in that direction from the edge of the bank complex. There was light from torches and the beat of a drum that helped lead me to the spot. So I got to the edge of a clearing where I stopped to check out what was going on."

"You're making this up, right?" said Seth.

"No, I am not," I said. "Hear me out. The top brass at The Bank was gathered in the clearing. By the way, none of our dads were there. All the hotshot managers were wearing these colorful ceremonial robes. Webb Dunn was there, too, with his badass security detail. Lucien Farr addressed them all from a podium up on a stage. He started talking about a breach in security at The Bank. So they bring out Tyler Morrison. He was handcuffed with plastic tie wraps."

"What?" said Frankie.

"Farr was reading him the riot act," I said, "about being the culprit at the bottom of the security issue. The next thing I know, spotlights were switched on around a lagoon that was back from the stage. Then the security guys drag Morrison over to the lagoon, cut off the tie wraps, and throw him in. A whole lot of alligators tore...him...up."

Seth got an enraged look about him and slammed me backwards, pinning me to the side of the van with both hands. "Tell me this is not fucking true, Bennie," he yelled.

"I'm telling you what I saw," I said. "It was terrible...it was awful."

"What the hell?" said Frankie.

"Look," said Seth, letting go of me, "I know Tyler. I know him well. We've gone out and had a few beers before. I even showed him around Sanibel when he first started working at The Bank. His cousin is Eddie Collins, who works with me."

"I didn't know you knew Tyler," I said. "And I didn't know he had a cousin working at The Bank.

"Neither did I," said Frankie.

"Well I don't tell you guys everything," said Seth. Then after a pause, "I cannot fucking believe this."

"It's the truth," I said, with a firm voice. "I was there. It happened."

As we got in the van and made the short drive up to The Edison, I proceeded to tell Seth and Frankie about meeting Garth, and how he helped get me out of what could have been big trouble. I told them about taking his boat across Pine Island Sound, and staying at his house. And I told them about Garth's uncle mysteriously disappearing. I told them everything I could think of.

We realized there was nothing to be done for the time being, so we decided to go ahead and spend a little time at the bar inside The Edison. But the spilling of my guts certainly put a damper on having any fun. Seth proceeded to get shit-faced at a rapid rate. It was his way of dealing with the subject. He really poured it on with multiple shots to go with his beers.

The evening came to an abrupt end when, on the way back from the restroom, Seth started to pick a fight with a guy who had accidentally bumped into him. Frankie and I saw the bad situation developing, so we quickly settled up at the bar and ushered Seth out of the establishment and to the van.

With Seth gradually passing out in the lounge chair in the back, I bounced some ideas off of Frankie while he safely drove us back to Sanibel. Thinking out loud during the ride, I suggested the three of us should take a road trip on Sunday over to St. James City for a visit with Garth. It seemed to me he would be helpful in talking things over. Being significantly older than the rest of us, I figured Garth would be the voice of reason. It sure seemed like we could use any guidance we could get.

"I'll call Garth tomorrow and set it up," I said.

"Count me in," said Frankie. "Road trip it is. Sounds like a good idea. I'd like to meet your friend. But, Ben, there is something I've never brought up when we have talked about The Bank. I guess this might as well be the time to tell you."

"What you got, Frankie?" I said. "No sense in holding back now."

"Did you ever wonder where The Bank gets its money?" said Frankie.

"Well," I said, "I know they keep making more and more money with their rip-off shenanigans with other banks. But, no, I never really thought about where the primary funds come from."

"Ready for this?" said Frankie. "The primary funds, as you put it, come from drug money."

"Really?" I said.

"Really," said Frankie. "It wasn't something I found out when I worked in Data Processing. I caught wind of it several times when I have driven Farr and some of the higher-ups to Page Field to fly out on the company jet. Man, that plane is a knockout. It's a Gulfstream G280. One time when they were going to be delayed taking off for a while, the pilot took me up inside it for a look."

"Right, right," I said, "you've told me before the airplane is cool. But what about the drug money?" I had to get Frankie back from the la-la land he would go to whenever he started talking about any stylish form of transportation. And it didn't matter what form of transportation it was. He loved them all.

"Oh…yeah," he said, snapping back to the subject. "Well, by piecing together some of their conversations and also noticing the flight plan in the cockpit that time, The Bank's other location is on Andros Island.

"Is that in the Bahamas?" I said.

"Yes, it is the largest island in the Bahamas. And one of the closer ones to South Florida. It's relatively undeveloped considering its size. I did a little research and found it has the largest tract of unexplored land in the Caribbean. And the Bahamas as a whole is one of the most prosperous countries in the world—and is tops in the Caribbean. They have great success with tourism and financial institutions."

"So, go on, go on, Frankie, about The Bank," I said.

"Several times in the limo I've heard them use the term black money. That means money that is not subject to taxes. Now, black money could mean any number of various tax shelters in the Bahamas or the Cayman Islands. But once I heard them say the name, Sanchez, when they were talking. It's no secret that Sanchez is head of one of the biggest drug cartels in Latin America."

"Wow," I said, "this is pretty deep."

"Very deep," said Frankie. "The line was something like, 'Sanchez dumped in ten million yesterday.' I just never wanted to bring this up to anybody before—even to you and Sleeping Beauty back there. But after what you said earlier about what happened, I had to let it out. So, anyway, how did you catch wind of all that going down?"

"Uh, I know someone in D/P," I said. "I guess you could say it got leaked to me. For now, I'd like to leave it at that." I decided to skip bringing up Gwen's name quite yet. I hadn't even told her about what had happened, and I thought it best to leave her name out of it for a while longer.

"So be it, my friend," said Frankie. "Looking forward to the road trip on Sunday."

10

Since Gwen had been away the previous weekend, we were both looking forward to spending some intimate time together—more than just a few hours at a bar during the week. We made plans to go back over to Fort Myers Beach again and stay at the Silver Sands Villas. We had enjoyed such a great weekend there before, and it was the closest beach off of Sanibel. Plus, we both felt safe we wouldn't be seen by anyone from The Bank. Not quite hiding in plain sight, but close.

I did tell her we had to make a fairly early getaway on Sunday morning, because I was going with my housemates to visit a friend on Pine Island. Gwen had no problem with that since she had some catching up to do from being away.

I had been mulling over what I was going to do about telling Gwen the gruesome details of that night. Every time I thought about it, I got a painful knot in the upper part of my stomach. After much agonizing, I realized I couldn't do it yet. After all, she worked in her uncle's department and lived in his house. I cared for Gwen to the point that I wanted to protect her at all costs.

My take on it was that I was willing to deceive her for the time being for her own good. Even though her uncle had framed Tyler Morrison, I didn't think he was the final decision maker on ordering the death sentence. I didn't want to put Gwen under the burden of thinking her uncle was a murderer. Although he was certainly an accessory to murder. To tell her, would be creating a no-win situation.

While we were over on Fort Myers Beach, my stress level went way down. Since I had reached a point of firm resolve on the subject, it allowed me to concentrate solely on Gwen. And what a great time we had. We took walks on the beach, hung around the pool at Silver Sands, and had several tasty dinners. Furthermore, we enjoyed each other with enthusiastic passion.

On Sunday, we checked out of the Silver Sands by mid-morning. We grabbed coffee and a pastry for the short ride back to Sanibel. After dropping Gwen at her car, I went back to the house on Dinkins Lake. When I arrived, Frankie was milling about the kitchen.

"So, what is the schedule for the trip today?" said Frankie.

"I told Garth we would be to his place around one-thirty."

"Well, I checked Google Maps on my phone," said Frankie, "and you are not going to believe the distance to St. James City from here."

"Riding in Garth's boat," I said, "it didn't take us long at all to go across Pine Island Sound."

"I checked that distance, too," he said. "Going straight over on the water, it can't be much more than a couple of miles from the back of Ding Darling to St. James City. Are you ready for this? From our house to there is about fifty-eight or fifty-nine miles."

"Wow," I said. "That is pretty amazing."

"I think we should allow an hour and a half for the drive."

"Sounds good to me," I said. "Let's leave by noon. Is Seth up yet?"

"No," said Frankie, "he's still hibernating. I'll go roust our boy."

Frankie came up with the brilliant idea of grabbing some lunch from The Over Easy Café for the ride. He called ahead and we picked up sandwiches and iced tea on our way. Seth was still about half asleep, so he asked Frankie to drive his van on the way to St. James City. As usual, I felt more relaxed with Frankie behind the wheel.

Since Frankie had a GPS app on his phone for locating addresses, I had him type in the address on Garth's business card. I had only been there once, and had come and gone via his boat through the canal. Getting the directions made finding it a lot easier than riding around looking for the unique-style house.

The trip to St. James City was uneventful. We drove all the way up Summerlin to Colonial and took the Midpoint Bridge over the Caloosahatchee River to Cape Coral. We made a left on Pine Island Road and cruised slowly through the funky little village of Matlacha. Lots of art galleries and other brightly-painted, eclectic shops. With all the structures sitting close to the narrow two-lane road, it has a small town feel. We all got a kick out of the sign that states Matlacha's slogan: "A Drinking Village with a Fishing Problem."

When we eventually came to a four-way stop, we turned left and drove eight or nine miles south on Stringfellow Road where we turned off on York Road. When we pulled up to Garth's house on the left, it was confirmed I'd been right about easily recognizing it. The A-frame structure was one-of-a-kind compared to all the other houses. As we walked to the door, Garth came out on the front deck to greet us.

"Garth," I said, "this is Seth and Frankie."

"Hey there, chums," said Garth. "Come on

into the air-conditioning and we'll sit for a bit."

Garth had stocked his refrigerator full of beer, and we each had a few while we talked…each of us except Frankie, who nursed only one. Frankie knew he didn't have the capacity to go toe-to-toe on the beer with the rest of us, and he also respected the fact he would, no doubt, be driving us back home.

For a while, it was friendly banter and laughs until I brought up the subject we were all waiting to get to. "Garth," I said, "when I called you the other day, I mentioned that I told Seth and Frankie about what happened the night in the refuge. And that I told them about your strong suspicion the same thing happened to your uncle. I told them everything."

"Indeed you did," said Garth, with his gravelly voice. Then turning to the guys, "What we saw last weekend wasn't something you would want do for fun on a Friday night in the summertime."

"What I didn't tell you," I said, "was that Seth was friendly with the guy who died that night."

Seth straightened in his chair and barked, "I'm pissed off, and I wanna do something about it."

"Look, chum," said Garth, "I'm sure we would all like to do something about it, but what?" Then gesturing to me, "We go to the cops and tell them what this here guy and I saw, and what's going to happen? If the cops go in there and mill around the complex interviewing people, what the hell is going to happen? Nothing."

"We've talked about it, Garth," I said. "I told the guys that we don't have any concrete evidence."

"All it would do," said Garth, "is stir up a hornet's nest and get you chums in hot water, or worse." Then after a pause, "Tell you what, why don't we take a little ride in my boat up the canal to Woody's. They've got a shaded deck and some live music on Sunday afternoons. We've got to think on this whole deal some more, and work on coming up with some ideas."

We went out the back of the house and Garth hustled ahead of us to tend to his boat. Seth turned and lowered his volume, saying, "What's with his voice? Do you believe that?"

Frankie laughed and said, "It sounds like he tried swallowing a handful of roofing nails."

We boarded Garth's boat and took a short, leisurely ride up the canal to Woody's Waterside. It was a sharp contrast from the high-speed blasts Garth and I had taken across Pine Island Sound only a week earlier.

In the sunny August afternoon, we cruised slowly at no-wake speed for probably less than a mile. Garth docked the boat at Woody's and we went up on the deck where a solo guy was providing some musical entertainment. The four of us took a table in the shade and ordered a pitcher of beer. When it arrived and we all had a full mug, Garth raised his and said, "Cheers. Here's to the people we've lost to those bastards."

After we toasted and each took a healthy gulp, Garth continued, "Look, chums, I'm as pissed as any of you about what's going on over there in the refuge. But it's going to take a commitment from you guys on the inside if we can manage to do something about it."

"We have to do something about it," said Seth. "I'm all in. For starters, let's do a shot in honor of the cause."

Frankie and I declined, but Seth and Garth each had a shot of vodka delivered with the second pitcher. About an hour later, and after Seth and Garth had toasted another shot together, a female's voice squealed from behind me, "Garth Milner, you old rascal. Fancy seeing you here."

A woman, maybe in her early forties, with long hair and wearing a peasant dress, went over to Garth and they hugged. It was what is known in these parts as the warm-weather, A-frame, hug. Everybody here sweats when they are outdoors in the summer. It is a given. But you get used to it, and no one has to apologize for their damp skin.

"Hey, chums," said Garth, "this is Miss Katy Monroe, newspaper writer extraordinaire. She never met a story she couldn't crush. Getting something past Katy is like trying to throw a pork chop past a bulldog. She wrote a nice profile of me a few years back, didn't you, Miss Katy?"

She smiled and said, "Aw, that one was easy, Garth. Writing about you was no effort at all. It was before I started doing the more investigative stories."

Garth turned back to us saying, "Katy, here, used to write for the local weekly paper, but now she's up there in the stratosphere writing for the Fort Myers News-Press. She's gone big-time on me. Next stop, USA Today. Right, Miss Katy?"

"We'll see about that," she said, smiling.

We all introduced ourselves and Katy pulled up a stool to join us. It was becoming clear that the shots were affecting Garth. I felt sure he could drink beer for a long period of time with steady consistency, but the shots seemed to have spring-boarded things to another level. His deep, raspy voice was beginning to slur some words.

"Hey, Katy," said Garth, as his face brightened, "you want a story? I got a story for you."

"Garth," I said, interrupting. "Not a good idea."

"Aw," said Garth, "Katy would be the perfect journalist to crack this here story."

Garth proceeded to tell Katy the basics of what had happened the night he and I unexpectedly met. He told her that Seth, Frankie, and I worked at The Bank. He also told her of his suspicions regarding the death of his uncle. Garth told her everything he knew. Of course, he didn't know of the inner workings of The Bank, which would have complicated matters even further. During his rambling, Frankie and I exchanged nervous glances over Garth's drunken disclosure.

Seth noticed nothing. With a glazed look in his eyes, he was preoccupied with staring at an inebriated girl who was dancing seductively by herself to the live music. She was wearing cutoff jean short-shorts and a bathing suit top.

Several times I tried to downplay the subject but Garth continued on. The clear issue was now murder, which is certainly not something to stifle. It was apparent Katy's interest was growing with each succeeding detail Garth growled out. As the conversation continued, and to my own amazement, I began to feel emboldened. We all had felt there was a need for some sort of action to generate justice. Maybe Katy could be the one to somehow help us, I thought.

"Well, guys," she said, "at this point, all you would be doing is sticking your necks out if you go to the police. It's your word against theirs without any solid evidence. I mean, I know the Assistant Chief of Police on Sanibel, but I can't go to him with what would sound like a harebrained story. You have to get me something else I can sink my teeth into."

With a dead-serious look on his face, Frankie said, "How about some recorded conversations?"

"That would help," said Katy.

"Now," I said, "how the heck do you propose we get these recorded conversations?"

With a calm voice and a straight face, Frankie said, "We bug Farr's office and the conference room, for starters."

"Now you're talking," said Katy.

"Look." I said, turning to Katy, "you are going to have to give us some time to figure things out. But as long as this is out in the open with you, there is more to tell. Garth doesn't even know about this. On top of what he has told you, and beyond the ruthless way The Bank deals with other world financial institutions, the foundation of its monetary funds comes from illegal drug money."

"This is getting more interesting by the minute," said Katy.

Maintaining his stern expression, Frankie chimed in, "It's laundered through an offshore satellite location on Andros Island in the Bahamas. A lot of money comes from a drug cartel in Latin America."

"Sort of like an old-fashioned, secret Swiss bank account," said Katy.

"Something like that," said Frankie. "Only in this case, The Bank is holding all the cards. They are using untaxed money to finance an operation that is probably violating all kinds of other international banking laws. And on top of that, they are killing people. It can only be a matter of time before they get busted from one direction or another."

"Well," said Katy, with a smile, "let's see if we can get the ball rolling on getting them busted."

At what seemed an appropriate time, I suggested we settle up and head back to Garth's house.

During much of our conversation with Katy, Seth had been up and gyrating with the rough-edged girl. She had been doing a good rendition of drunk, dirty dancing. Frankie went over and pried Seth away, escorting him back to our table.

Soaked in sweat, Seth insisted that he and Garth do one last shot, to which Garth agreed. While all the activity was going on, Katy gave me her business card and, with a wink, suggested we all keep in touch. We finally said goodbyes and made our way down to Garth's boat.

Frankie and I stayed on the dock to help untie the ropes to the boat. Seth stumbled onboard, almost losing his balance. As drunk as I knew Garth was, I was amazed at how he immediately had his sea legs when he boarded. It seemed almost by instinct he took charge and gave us clear instructions for shoving off.

Although it was a hot, sunny August afternoon, a gusty breeze had started kicking up and there was a row of dark clouds in the eastern sky. During the short trip back down the canal, Garth held a steady line and maintained a no-wake speed. I guess his years of experience paid off with stable control even in his affected state.

When we got to his house, Garth performed a perfect docking of the boat. It could not have been done in a more calm and precise manner. However, there was an instantaneous reversal in his condition once he shut off the motor and climbed up on his dock. He turned around to lend a hand to Seth who was having trouble with his footing, and the two of them ended up sprawled arm-in-arm down onto the dock. They both broke out with hearty laughs as Garth slurred, "One of us is drunk."

Frankie and I secured the boat to the pilings while Seth and Garth struggled to their feet. It became just a matter of herding them into the house. Cooler heads prevailed and our stay was very brief. As we were going out the front door, Garth stopped me and, with glassy eyes and some slurring in his coarse voice, said, "Say, chum, I guess I got a little carried away today with spilling the beans to Katy. But I'm fed up and frustrated. If you chums can figure out a plan for where things go from here, I'm in with you. I can't do much from the outside, but I'm telling you I'm in with you."

When we got to the van, Seth wobbled his way through the side door and plopped down on the recliner in back. Frankie got behind the wheel and I rode shotgun. It was the same seating arrangement we had on the drive to Garth's, but on the return trip Seth was passed out within the first ten minutes.

11

As we drove, Frankie had music on the radio but he and I had not spoken for a while. I think we both realized everything about The Bank was becoming a more complex predicament, and we were feeling the pressure of being at the heart of it.

After we exchanged several quick, serious glances, Frankie finally said, "Ben, I hadn't opened up on stuff about The Bank until today, except with you. And I have to say I feel better talking about it. Ever since that short period of time I worked in Data Processing and dealt with the investment guys, I've been holding some things in. But knowing what you, and Seth, and now Garth have gone through makes me feel motivated to do something that will make the wrongs of The Bank come to an end."

"Well," I said, "what kind of things do you mean, Frankie?"

"There was a young investment guy who had a wife and a couple of kids. He was driven to succeed, like all those guys are. He told me he worked as hard as he could. But he was feeling the pressure to excel both from the Bank and from home. Over the course of several months I could see it aging him. Then one day he wasn't around anymore. A gal in the department who knew him told me the story being circulated was he was supposed to be taking some time off. But she had heard from a friend that the guy committed suicide."

"Really?" I said.

"Yeah," said Frankie. "Apparently he went to a golf course in Fort Myers one night, sat on a bench at one of the tees and blew his brains out. The groundskeepers found him when they were mowing early the next morning. Guess he couldn't take it anymore."

"Man," I said, "that's bad."

As we were crossing the Caloosahatchee River from Cape Coral to Fort Myers on the Midpoint Bridge, we were going straight into a gusting wind. Frankie did a good job handling the van as it was buffeted about. The earlier line of dark clouds was now almost over us and had taken on an eerie charcoal color.

After we crossed the bridge and had gone only a mile or two down Summerlin, it started pouring. Huge drops of rain pounded down, making visibility difficult. I felt confident in Frankie's driving, but both sets of our eyes were focused on what little we could see ahead. Seth was doing us no good at all. He was still in sleep mode despite the rain, wind, and booming thunder.

"It's best to slow down," said Frankie, over the clamor of the downpour pelting the van, "but I don't like to pull over and stop. There's a chance somebody will run right up your butt. And the worst thing to do is put on the four-way flashers and keep going. Only should use them if you do decide to stop."

"I'm with you, Frankie," I said. "I think you're doing a good job."

"One thing I like to do when I am out on the interstate," said Frankie, "is to get behind a tractor-trailer, and keep a decent following distance no matter how slow they are going. It's like having a big offensive lineman blocking for you."

By the time we got to the Sanibel Causeway, we had driven out of the storm. Crossing the tall bridge and looking toward the Gulf, it was sunny and beautiful. Anyone seeing what was now ahead of us would not believe what we had just driven through. That is unless they turned around and looked at the darkness behind.

"Now that we are past the rain crisis," I said, "there is something I haven't told you or anybody else, including the load sitting behind us."

"Go on," said Frankie.

"Most of the information I've been offering has come from a girl I'm seeing who works in Data Processing. Her name is Gwen Copeland, and we've been spending a lot of time together recently. You wouldn't have known her in that office since you transferred out over a year ago."

"No, I don't know her," said Frankie, "but I know who you mean. A while back, one of the guys pointed her out to me in the café. And now that you mention it, I have noticed you've been missing in action quite a bit on weekends and some nights of the week."

"Yeah," I said, "and it's on the verge of being very serious. I guess that is why I haven't shared anything about her with you guys. It's a conflict. We all know how it is at The Bank. Everyone is paranoid about practically everyone else. And if you care about somebody, guy or gal, you want to try to protect them from getting in any trouble."

"That is for sure, sir," said Frankie.

"But here is the biggie," I said. "Gwen's uncle, Harris Copeland, set up Morrison to be taken out."

"I know Harris Copeland," said Frankie. "He was the manager of D/P when I worked in there."

"Well," I said, "Gwen told me she overheard her uncle's drunken tirade to himself one night. He planned it out to frame Morrison because he feared the guy as an up-and-coming hotshot. By the way, Copeland was there that night in the refuge."

"So does Gwen know about what happened?" asked Frankie.

"No," I said. "I haven't worked up the guts to tell her. Even though she lives in a separate wing of his house, I can't bring myself to tell her she's living under the same roof with a murderer—or at least close to that."

"I think you're doing the right thing," said Frankie, "at least for now."

When we got back to the house, I shook Seth back to consciousness and aimed him in the direction of the open, side door of the van. It was clear that for the balance of the afternoon and evening he would be unproductive. Frankie and I spent some time sitting on the front porch kicking around ideas on how to carry out our general plan to acquire taped conversations of Farr and his inner circle of associates.

"It's going to be difficult," said Frankie, "to get into Farr's office and the conference room next door."

"Next to impossible, I'd say. The only reason I was in there was because we were painting."

"It would probably be better," said Frankie, "if we could get up into the open space above those offices. That way it would be easier to hide the little transmitters in the top of the fluorescent light fixtures that hang on the ceiling below. Look, I've never bugged anything before, but I'm willing to try."

"Yes," I said, "there is a low attic above the offices. It is where all of the utilities are run. Electric, water, air-conditioning ducts...really everything except the sewer. It's about the height of a crawl space in the basements up north."

In an instant, a bright light went on in my head..."Wait a minute, wait a minute, a couple of weeks ago I supervised a crew that did some repair work in the foyer of the administration building where Farr's office is. There had been a water leak in the roof that had worked its way down to the ceiling. I was up on the roof and I also poked my head up though the access panel to the attic area. It is in an alcove off the foyer."

"Maybe that job needs a little follow-up inspection?" said Frankie.

"Bingo," I said. "There is not much activity going on during the weekend. Probably only a guard coming around every now and then. And there are not any surveillance cameras up in the attics of any of the buildings. They are all outside and in the offices and hallways."

"I am going to get on the Internet," said Frankie, "and do a little shopping for, shall we say, some covert listening equipment. I'll see how quickly we can have a kit shipped here to us. Never studied up on that type of product before, but I'm a pretty quick learner."

"That you are, Frankie," I said. "I am thinking out loud here, but doing it on a Saturday would be best. I could tell the guard we were on our way out for the day, and I just wanted to stop by and double check the issue on the roof and above the ceiling of the foyer. It will make me look like I am super thorough."

"Yeah," said Frankie, smiling, "you sure are efficient. And we will bring along the big guy who is passed out in there, too. If it is needed, he would be the perfect candidate to distract the guard. You are Mr. Efficiency and he is Mr. Entertainment."

"He is indeed," I said, laughing. "I'll say I am having you go up and crawl around in the attic because you are smaller and more nimble than me."

I could see a brightening spark of enthusiasm in Frankie's eyes as he said, "Since you are bringing with you the Assistant Food and Beverage Manager, and a driver in the Transportation Department, it will look like you just swung by with your buddies to check on some work you were responsible for in the first place."

"We will take Seth's van," I said, "and bring along a flashlight and whatever other tools you think we will need. I can get the tall stepladder from the maintenance shop in the next building. Think about that foresight by the bigwigs. They have the maintenance area located close to the administration building so that a problem can be fixed as quickly as possible."

"Yup," said Frankie, "don't they just have it all figured out. But no need to worry about a flashlight, Ben. I have a light I can wear on my head. It is like a smaller version of a miner's light those guys wear on their helmets. I use it sometimes when I'm working on my car. It is great because it keeps both hands free. And I have a tool belt to carry any other stuff I need. Come to think of it, I will bring along a hand-held vacuum. I can set it up running right where I am working. Don't want to have any drywall dust falling down onto the conference room table or Farr's desk."

"And I will get the blueprints for that building from the Facilities Management office, so you will know when you are over the middle of those rooms. I can figure the distance from the ceiling access to the location of the light fixtures."

"I have a fifty-foot tape," said Frankie.

"That should be plenty of length," I said. "Those offices are in the middle of the building. I don't think it would be more than fifty feet."

"If it is further when you check it on the blueprint," said Frankie, "I will bring along another twenty-five-foot tape. That is not a problem. I can make it work."

"There needs to be some fine tuning," I said, "but I think the plan we are working on is a good start. We just need to get some more pieces of the puzzle. And by the way, we will split up the cost of the equipment."

"That is fine," said Frankie, with a laugh, "but it is not a big deal, seeing as how we all probably make two or three times as much money for what we do at The Bank compared to what we would get out in the real world. We should start thinking like The Bank and act like money is no object."

We bantered about some more possible ideas for a while and then Frankie retired inside to do some research on the bugging equipment. He told me to just think of the device as a glorified baby monitor system, which also had the capability of recording. If Frankie was figuring out something technical, I felt confident we were on the right track.

I knew I absolutely had to keep this next course of action entirely away from Gwen. It seemed like the list of things to hide from her was growing. It was not my nature to act that way with people in general, and especially not someone I was close to. But I was determined it was the way it should be for the time being. And the situation was made particularly stressful when I considered the possibility of a negative outcome. If what we were planning was discovered at any point by the higher powers of The Bank, I was sure it would ticket the three of us to a destiny in the Gator Lagoon.

I sat on the porch for a while and daydreamed through an endless, swarming beehive of possible outcomes to what we were considering. I was thankful for the interruption to that agonizing thought process when Frankie stormed out of the house with a handful of notes.

Plunking back down on his chair, he said, "Okay, here is what I found out. There are lots of types of bugging devices—hardwire, radio frequency, optical, and acoustic. But the newest one is a GSM bug. They are referred to as infinity transmitters. I think the one that would be best to use is called the GSM Bug Long Life. It is voice-activated and has six weeks of battery life. There is no way I am going to try hardwiring anything with the short amount of time we will have."

"Six weeks ought to be plenty of time," I said. "If we can't get some good stuff from it by then, it is not going to happen. And speaking of the short time you were talking about, it is going to be about a thousand degrees up in that attic. It is August after all."

"Thanks for mentioning that," said Frankie, with a sarcastic smile. Then turning back to his notes, "I am also ordering a digital recorder we can set up here at the house. We are only about a mile and a half from the complex, but this has a limitless distance anyway. It works like a phone, and the recorder has four hundred hours of recording time. It has an ear plug I can use to listen to the recordings. I think I will probably type out and print a transcript of the recorded conversations. It would be easier for us to be able to read it. If I can't figure out which voice is which, you and Seth can listen to see who you think is speaking. Setting up a camera in the ceilings of the offices for video recording would be much more difficult, and bigger."

"I think the voices should be fairly easy," I said. "We know for sure the only woman's voice will be that sweet Ava Branstein."

"And I have heard Webb Dunn's voice in my sleep," said Frankie. "I am going to go ahead and order everything. It is coming from England, but if I pay extra it can be here in about a week."

"So how much does this all cost?" I asked.

"Everything we need," said Frankie, "plus the shipping, should be around four hundred."

"We will split it up, like I said."

Frankie laughed and said, "It is a small price to pay to get some juicy information."

As he went back into the house, my apprehensions of earlier faded. I was encouraged by Frankie's enthusiasm and confidence. And when it came to Seth, I could tell by his previous fired-up outbursts that he would be willing to pitch in wherever needed. I was feeling a youthful eagerness to take a stand and follow through with something that needed to be done. Between the three of us, I felt like we had a good team. Damn it, we are going to do this, I thought.

12

Since the bugging equipment would take a week to arrive, I made arrangements to spend the following weekend with Gwen. The weekdays dragged out to an excruciating length. Several days after work I went to the small gym at The Bank to either lift weights or run on the treadmill. The exercise helped me unwind both physically and mentally from the buildup of stress I was feeling about the upcoming project.

I met Gwen for drinks in the evening twice during the week. But just as before, those dates felt like short-lived teases compared to the passion-filled weekends we had shared together. We decided to stick with our standard plan of staying at the Silver Sands Villas on Fort Myers Beach. The convenience of the location, and the worlds-apart feel when compared to Sanibel made it a good choice. We both were still committed to keeping our relationship confidential. Frankie was the only other person at The Bank who was aware of it and, from what he had said to me, I felt certain the secret was safe with him. I knew I would also be telling Seth in due time.

Gwen and I got a late start on Friday evening because a job I was supervising ran past business hours. We managed to make it to the Silver Sands a little before nine, and then scooted across the street to the beach bar, Nemo's, for the aftermath of the sunset. We took a table on the beach side of the bar and toasted cold beers in honor of the view. The high cloud formations that night made for a spectacular palette of vibrant colors for many minutes after the sun had set.

"You can't buy something that natural and beautiful," I said.

"No," said Gwen, "you sure can't. But I bet some of the money-obsessed people at The Bank might try to buy it anyway."

I had been tight-lipped with Gwen about events at The Bank during the recent times we had been together. But I felt sure enough of her true concerns about the wrongs she knew were being committed to bring her a little more up to date. And although I had no intention of mentioning what the guys and I were planning to do, I thought she might be able to provide some insight from the financial end of things.

"A little while back," I said, "Frankie brought up some information about The Bank that I had no idea about. He said a big source of the funding comes from drug money."

With a surprised look on her face, Gwen said, "I didn't know that either."

"Frankie caught wind of it several times when he was chauffeuring Farr and a couple of others to Page Field for a flight on the corporate jet. He said there is a satellite location for The Bank on Andros Island in the Bahamas, and the deposits are made there."

"Well," said Gwen, "that would explain this large account we have in Data Processing. It is designated by just the letters, A.I.—guess that stands for Andros Island. It has the most transactions of any of the accounts. Most of the other ones are earmarked for activity in London where we have interactions with world banks." Then after a pause she added, "Drug money. Unbelievable."

"Yeah," I said, "between overheard conver-sations in the limo, and one time when Frankie saw the flight plan for the corporate jet, he is sure of it."

Clearing her throat in a good-humored way, Gwen said, "Having had a double major in Business and Economics at Skidmore, I think I can offer some knowledge of the fine art of money laundering, since that is apparently what is going on. I actually had a course that dealt with such types of illegal activity, if you can believe it. I guess they wanted us to learn what *not* to do in our business lives."

"I am all ears," I said.

"This sounds like what is known as bulk cash smuggling. It means physically smuggling cash from wherever the drug dealers get it, and then depositing it in a financial institution in another jurisdiction. In this case, it must be a commercial bank that The Bank has somewhere on Andros Island. The advantage is the simple fact that the Bahamas have less rigorous enforcement of banking laws. It provides for greater secrecy and reduced taxation all the way around. Come to think of it, you could say our salaries at The Bank are black salaries. The ridiculously large amount we are paid for what we do is actually dirty money. Dirty and black are really interchangeable terms for untaxed money."

"Frankie also used the term, black money," I said, smiling. "I will definitely think about that the next time I get my paycheck."

"So," she said, "The Bank is not reporting these cash transactions. I often wondered why there is this constant transferring of funds in my office. Now it makes sense. The money is being moved though a series of accounts to hide its true source. And the high daily volume of wire transfers makes it difficult for any enforcement agency to trace the transactions."

"The Bank has it all figured out, huh?" I said.

"When they move these untraceable funds," said Gwen, "into the real financial world, the money gets mixed with funds that have legitimate origins. It makes it even more complex to uncover."

"Brilliant," I said.

After all of the color in the sky had gone dark, we decided to call it an early evening. As we were about to cross Estero Boulevard, the sound of live music could be heard coming from the Cottage Bar. Under other circumstances, the music might have drawn us to enjoy some entertainment. But we both had more pressing priorities, namely each other. Gwen had a tight squeeze on my hand as we walked to the motel. I was tingling with excited eagerness by the time we reached our room.

The next morning, after coffee and bagels, we took a long walk on the beach. The standard humidity of summer mornings was in the air, but a nice breeze off the Gulf made our walk more than bearable. There was an extended quiet period of time between us until Gwen said, "It is just so different for both of us when we are together and not at The Bank. I wish it could be like this a whole lot more."

"I feel the same way, Gwen. It would have been nice if we knew each other in college. Tell me some more about your years at Skidmore. I've always heard it is very exclusive."

"Look who's talking," said Gwen, "you went to Penn. That is Ivy League, Mister."

"Let's just say we both had the benefit of a good education," I said. "And, at The Bank, we have also benefited from who we are related to."

"True, on both counts," said Gwen. "Okay, Skidmore College. It was founded in the early 1900s as a women's school. It wasn't until 1971 that men were admitted. And the enrollment is still about sixty percent women."

"Even more reason why I should have gone there instead of Penn."

"Funny boy," said Gwen. "I think the overall enrollment is a little under twenty-five hundred. And most of my classes had only fifteen or twenty students."

"That makes it a select few who get accepted, I bet."

"Right," said Gwen. "The acceptance rate is somewhere under ten percent."

"Wow," I said. "So did you get into any activities when you were there?"

"I was on the riding team," she said, "and did a lot of skiing with a small club."

"As in horseback riding?"

"Yes," said Gwen, "as in horseback riding. It's an intercollegiate sport at Skidmore. After all, the school mascot is the Thoroughbreds. Although that is probably because the school is so close to the Saratoga Race Course, not because of show riding like I did. I had done quite a bit of riding when I was growing up. And I got some scholarship money from Skidmore because of it. I guess you could say they recruited me. I do miss it, though. I would like to get back into riding. I love it. Being down here, and with work, it just hasn't happened. How about you? What sort of extra things did you do at Penn?"

"Well," I said, "I had played baseball all through high school. But I wasn't viewed as being good enough to get a baseball scholarship at Penn. I did try out for the team and made the squad my freshman year. I didn't get in very many games. Unfortunately, I could see the handwriting on the wall with other players in my class that were on the team. I would have ended up sitting behind the same guys the rest of the way through school. So I played some intramural softball, but I never liked it as much as baseball. If it wasn't for living down here, and with all the commitments at The Bank, I would try to hook up with a Semi-Pro team up north in the summer. I still think I'm good enough to play. But it would take a little while to get my timing back."

On the return walk up the beach, the pelicans were heavily into their morning feeding session. In one area offshore, six or eight of them were repeatedly dive bombing into the surf. It is amazing the accuracy pelicans have in grabbing fish out of the Gulf in a high-speed dive. The group we watched gorged themselves. We got to see nature at work right before our eyes.

Gwen's voice took on a more serious tone as she said, "Ben, I know there is a good thing going on between us—there is no doubt about that. But the last few times we've been together I've sensed you have been holding back about something. I sure hope it is about work, and not about me. What gives?"

In an instant, the thought flashed through my mind that she had noticed some kind of change I had been trying hard to suppress. I quickly decided the deception should not go on any longer if we were really going to stay as close as we were. But, for her sake, I chose to leave out the gory details of the Gator Lagoon.

"Look, Gwen," I said, "I have strong feelings toward you. And I have been keeping some things inside because I don't want to upset you in any way."

"Ben," she said, "I grew up on Long Island. I've spent time in New York City. I have been around some brusque people in my life. I think I am tougher than you are giving me credit for."

I paused and took a deep breath before saying, "You know all the things we have discussed about The Bank? Well, it's even worse yet. Tyler Morrison is no longer alive. The top brass did away with him."

"It can't be. How do you know this?"

"Just believe me," I said. "I know it for sure, and it is not the first time it has happened. They have their ways to eliminate anybody who they see as a threat."

With a resigned look on her face, Gwen said, "So Uncle Harris is at the bottom of this." It came across more as a statement than a question.

"I suppose he is, especially based on what you heard from him that night. But that's not to say he issued the orders."

"In a strange way this doesn't surprise me," she said. "Uncle Harris has always seemed to have an underlying nasty streak in him that I could never put my finger on. It has been stilted and uncomfortable at times living in the same house with him. It was only at my father's urging that I'm working at The Bank in the first place. They *are* brothers. My dad knew I could make great money right out of college. Plus, my aunt is also uncomfortable to deal with. I think she resents me being young and independent, with a good job."

"Look," I said, "I know this whole thing is a bad situation…it can't be ignored. I've talked with Frankie and Seth, and we all agree there has to be justice. We know we don't have enough evidence to go to the police yet. So we are going to try to get some more information."

"This sounds like trouble," said Gwen.

"But," I said, "if we all just stand by and don't do anything, it is like we are accepting it—even condoning it. This is entirely up to you, but if you can find anything from your office that would be of assistance, it would be helpful to the cause."

"Ordinarily," said Gwen, "if something like this came up, I would be the first person to try to discourage you. I do not want to see you putting yourself in danger. But now knowing all that I do, I'm angry, and I want to help if I can. This is all so very wrong."

"It is exactly the way the guys and I feel," I said. "We want the bad guys, whoever they are, to face the consequences."

"Count me in," she said with a smile.

"Now, Gwen," I said, "for the rest of today

and tomorrow while we are together, how about if we try to put all this on the back burner. Let's concentrate on each other."

"Sold," she said, as she hugged and kissed me hard.

A weight had been lifted off me with the talk we'd had. I felt so much better about not having to deceive her any longer. Except for the details of the gruesome event I had witnessed, I knew I could be open and honest with Gwen. It was evident she was feeling a call to action like the rest of us. But I conveniently left out telling her about the forthcoming venture to plant the bugs in Farr's office and conference room. I figured it would be better to let her in on it after we had some solid facts.

The balance of the day consisted of alternating sessions of passionate interludes in our room and relaxing stints by the pool. After an outstanding seafood dinner at Matanzas Inn, we walked back toward our motel. As we passed the Surf Club bar, we saw a live band playing on the outside deck. The music sounded remarkably good, so we took a table for a nightcap.

We found out from the waitress that the group was called Habitat for Harmony. It was a catchy name. The band consisted of two men and two women, all appearing to be middle-aged. The voices, the harmonies, the percussion, the tightness of the group, all were outstanding. But beyond that, there was a certain upbeat chemistry between them. As Gwen and I watched and listened, I thought about being older, maybe for one of the first times. I thought about being like the members of the band, not in their musical talent, but in their youthful spirit. And it felt good wanting to be like that and feel like that. Considering the forthcoming risks to be taken, in the back of my mind I was also wondering if Gwen, the guys, and I would all even make it to middle-age.

13

On Tuesday of the following week, we received the package with the bugging equipment. Frankie said he wanted an evening or two to study up on the user guide. We decided that Thursday evening, instead of going out, would be a planning session at the house. I picked up a case of beer and Seth bought two large pizzas. I was sure he had earmarked one of them for himself. Then it was down to business.

Frankie called the meeting to order and said, "I took the liberty of also buying a multiple-feed personal radio system. It has a four-person capacity with a single ear bud for each that is practically invisible. I thought we could use it this Saturday when we plant the bugs in the administration building. And, it might come in handy down the road."

"Frankie," I said, "How much do we owe you for all this stuff?"

"The radio system," said Frankie, "was a little over two-fifty. And the bugging equipment and shipping was right at four hundred. If you guys each give me two hundred, I'll take care of the rest. I just had to get this radio system."

"No problem," said Seth.

"Fine," I said. I was thinking Frankie probably paid more than two-fifty for the radio stuff. But since he had made the decision to buy it, he was going to cover the extra expense. It was his way of operating.

Then Frankie continued, "I will activate the battery on the GSM Bug Long Life on Saturday morning before we go over to the complex. And we will also test out the personal radio system. The single ear bud speaker is so sensitive that the person wearing it can just barely whisper and it is audible to the other feeds. Basically, it's able to override other nearby conversations."

The three of us all arose Saturday morning with the excited anticipation of a secret mission. Frankie activated the battery on the bugging device, and we successfully tested out the radio system. As Frankie had told us, the ear bud was very small and was virtually unnoticeable. Our trial run to check how it worked proved you could whisper ever so quietly and it was understandably heard by the other two guys. Even when we had Seth stand near me and talk loud gibberish, Frankie could clearly hear in his ear bud what I whispered. It was a heck of a sophisticated apparatus.

Seth drove us in his van and we entered Wildlife Drive through the exit gate of Ding Darling.

He then waved and greeted the guard who opened the sliding camouflaged gate at the trail to The Bank compound. It wasn't at all unusual for any of the three of us to be coming in on a Saturday.

As we were unloading various equipment we needed from the van, Frankie did an unscheduled final check of our radio system by whispering, "I sure hope these offices we are bugging don't have any recording detection devices." Seth and I gave each other a blank look until Seth said, "Knock it off, Frankie. Let's go."

We grabbed a six-foot step ladder from the maintenance area and went into the lobby of the administration building. I spoke to the security guard as the guys set up the ladder beneath the ceiling access in the corner alcove, "Just here to check on the roof and ceiling repair one of my crews did in here a little while back."

"Go right ahead," he said.

Seth proceeded to engage the guard in idle conversation in the lobby. Putting on a large tool belt that held the bugging equipment, a cordless drill, and a small hand-held vacuum, Frankie hoisted himself into the attic crawl space area. I positioned myself on the ladder with my head stuck through the access opening. Frankie wore the miner's cap light on his forehead, and I helped by holding one end of the measuring tape. With my other hand, I cast some additional light toward Frankie's direction with a large flashlight.

The heat in the crawl space was almost unbearable. And I only had my head up in the attic.

Frankie had assured me he had properly hydrated with water and sport drinks earlier. But I knew it was going to be a yeoman effort on his part to move about and do his job without wilting.

When Frankie had gone twenty or thirty feet, I decided to check on him. "How are you doing?" I asked.

"So far, so good," he said in a low voice. "But man, it's a little on the warm side up here."

He stopped to check the length on the tape, looked at the small blueprint of the attic area, made a slight adjustment in his direction, and crawled on. He finally stopped and did another check of the plan. "Okay," he said, "I'm over the center light fixture in Farr's office. I'll do this one, and then I'll have to use the other tape measure to get over to the conference room. The one we are holding is at forty-seven feet."

The minutes were agonizing. And although Seth was having a good verbal exchange, eventually the guard called up to me, "Is everything okay up there?"

Instinctively, I pretended to answer a request from Frankie by calling into the attic, "Alright, Frankie, I'll bring up the sealer."

I secured the tape at the edge of the access panel, set down the light, and scooted down the ladder. I grabbed a five-gallon bucket that held a caulk gun loaded with a tube of leak sealer, plus other tools. As I went up the ladder, I called back down toward Seth and the guard, "He found a couple of minor leak spots. We'll get them temporarily from the inside, and then I'll get a crew on the roof on Monday."

Just as I went up through the ceiling access, I heard Seth, using an energized voice, say to the guard, "Hey, pal, come on out and take a look at the new reel I got for my surf rod. It's in the van." That comment got the guard's attention and the two of them marched out the front door of the lobby. In his own way, Seth was doing his part to help pull off the operation we were conducting.

The heat in the attic was close to overwhelming. I shined the flashlight toward Frankie, who was crawling to the second location. "Are you okay, Frankie?" I asked. "It's ridiculous up here."

"You got that right," said Frankie. "I finished the one over Farr's office. One more to go."

"I'm bringing the bucket that has a couple bottles of water."

"Sure can use it," said Frankie. "You can pull the fifty-foot tape back in. I'm using the twenty-five footer to get to the conference room fixture. And I left the roll of duct tape near that first one. Bring it along."

"Got it," I said. When I made it to where Frankie was working, I was soaked completely through. With the beam from my flashlight, I could see Frankie was too.

He rose up on his knees and, with urgency, said, "Gotta have some water."

We each gulped down a pint bottle of water in an almost continuous flow. My eyes had begun to sting like mad from dripping sweat, but I was not going to waste any precious fluid I could drink to flush them out. I acted as Frankie's assistant as he finished securing the second bug.

By the time I put all of our assorted belongings in the bucket, Frankie was finished. He did one last pass with the hand-held vacuum over the small opening at the light fixture, and we were on our way out of the attic.

We scampered down the ladder, and although the air-conditioning in the lobby felt somewhat refreshing, we had other things on our mind. We burst out the front double doors of the building, and barged right into Seth and the guard who were on their way back in. Frankie and I were making a beeline to the van where we had the better half of a case of spring water. It was amazing that neither of us experienced any bloated feeling after guzzling several more bottles. I don't think the water stayed in our stomachs very long. It felt like it was flowing in a direct pipeline out of all the pores of our bodies.

Due to Frankie's slight weight and size, he had a few minutes where he felt lightheaded. In addition to the size issue, he had been up in the extreme heat longer than I had. I gave him some ice cubes to rub on the underside of his wrists. Then I soaked a cloth in the ice water of the cooler we had packed, and held it on the back of Frankie's neck. In a few minutes the combination of cooling and hydration brought his body temperature down, and helped him feel better.

"How are you doing, Frankie?" I asked.

"Coming around, coming around." Frankie perked up a little, and with a modest laugh, "I'd say we are two sweaty messes. Glad we brought along some dry clothes."

"Yeah," I said, "a shower over at the gym is going to feel mighty good. Are you sure you're alright?"

"Feeling much better." After a hesitation, he said, "The job is done...and I think I did it right. But we will have to wait until Monday to see if it works. Farr probably won't be in those offices, and talking to anyone, until then."

"I'm hoping it works, Frankie."

"Me, too," he said.

Seth collected all of our equipment from the lobby, and returned the ladder to the maintenance area while Frankie and I were in recovery mode at the van. Seth returned to the van with a broad smile, and said, "It's all good from my end. The guard, Donnie, was very interested in my fishing stuff. Glad I had my rod with the new reel here in the van. It helped to keep him distracted."

"Good thinking on the fly, Seth," I said. "It definitely bought us some time. Frankie thinks he nailed it."

"Way to go, man," boomed Seth.

"Hold on, hold on," said Frankie. "Let's remove these little transmitters we have in our ears, please. You're blowing out my eardrums."

Frankie placed the ear buds in their case, and we all headed to the gym, which was several buildings away. After we showered and changed, Seth declared that a celebration was in order. He thought the festivities should consist of lunch and beer. I suggested we get takeout from Bailey's General Store and go back to our house. I didn't think it was a good idea to go out to a bar or restaurant for several reasons. First, I didn't know how long Frankie would be able to hang in there before he would need to get some rest. It was apparent his energy level was still not back to normal. Second, and more importantly, I knew for sure we would want to talk about our freshly completed project. Being out in public and chatting it up, especially anywhere on Sanibel, would not be a wise plan.

When we returned to Seth's van, he got behind the wheel and cranked the air-conditioning full blast. I rode shotgun and Frankie kicked back in the recliner for the ride. It was role reversal for Seth and Frankie compared to most of the times when we were out and about. For a change, Seth was actually driving his own van while the three of us were together. I don't think Frankie was sound asleep on the ride to Bailey's, but he had his eyes closed and he didn't say anything.

When we got to Bailey's, I told Frankie to stay put in the van. Seth left it running with the A/C on. After we got inside, Seth insisted on paying for everything. He handed me thirty dollars and sent me over to the deli to order sandwiches. He said he would meet me at the van. I turned back to see Seth storming straight for the beer cooler.

As we drove back up Sanibel-Captiva Road, Seth and I toasted a beer. Normally, we didn't drink at all while we were driving. It is against Florida law to have an open alcohol container in a vehicle. At least when the three of us were out, we were consistent in abiding by those rules. So Seth and I did our best to be discreet and, anyway, it was a very unusual set of circumstances. Frankie said he would wait until we got back to the house. I think he knew he only had the capacity for a couple of beers before he would be doing some serious reclining. He was washed out, and for good reason.

We rehashed our operation over lunch and beers. Shortly thereafter, Frankie crashed on one of our two living room sofas and was asleep in no time. I was not far behind him on the other sofa. The last I saw Seth before I dozed off, he was planted in one of our overstuffed chairs watching golf on television with the sound low. He must have realized that his level of exertion from our morning's activities was not close to mine, or especially Frankie's, so he was being considerate of our taxed condition.

Later in the afternoon, I awoke to hear Seth in the kitchen filling a cooler with ice. Frankie was still sleeping. I got up, went to the kitchen sink, and splashed water on my face.

"What's going on, big guy?" I said.

"I came up with a last minute date," he said. "I hadn't planned anything ahead of time for tonight. I'm going to roll out of here in a few minutes."

It was no surprise Seth could arrange a spontaneous rendezvous with someone of the opposite sex. An impulsive request on his part for a date was typically met with availability and acceptance. That was the kind of appeal he had with girls.

"Look, Seth," I said, "I am not trying to

lecture you on this. But no matter how much fun you are having, or how much you have to drink, what we did is top secret. No leaks, okay?"

"Don't give it a second thought, Bennie," he said. "You know how I toe the line at The Bank. I am always solid with the program there. I can keep my social life and work very, very separate. What we are involved in now is nothing that goes any further. Believe me, I've got it."

I felt good about what Seth had said. I may well have been out of line by advising him about being cautious with his tongue. I couldn't ever remember Seth passing rumors or gossiping about anything having to do with work. It was just that when he was out partying, his behavior was so completely different in every way. Seth was a living example of the expression, "work hard, play hard." But in this case, I guess I had a compelling reason to have a guarded mindset about what we had done. If anything went awry, we all faced the most severe set of consequences.

14

The next day was a leisurely Sunday with Gwen. Following our normal plan, we met in the morning at the Olde Sanibel Shoppes and dropped off Gwen's car. We remained unified in our pattern of not wanting to be seen together on Sanibel. We thought it was still a good idea to not arouse any suspicion or interest.

We drove in my Jeep down through Fort Myers Beach and went to Lover's Key State Park, just to the south. Lover's Key is one of the most visited of all Florida state parks. After riding the small tram from the parking lot to the beach, we spent a couple of hours sunning until the late-summer heat got to both of us. Another time of year would have been better to linger in the rustic, naturally preserved surroundings. If it weren't for the large gazebo and the restrooms just behind us at the edge of the Gulf of Mexico, Gwen and I could have very well been relaxing on the same beach a hundred or more years ago. The park is that unspoiled.

We rode the tram back to the parking area and proceeded to take showers in the updated lavatory facilities. Then it was back up through Fort Myers Beach for lunch at Junkanoo, which is attached to Fresh Catch Bistro where we had dined before. Junkanoo is far more casual but has the same scenic view of the Gulf. We got a table at the window, ordered drinks, and watched some friendly coed volleyball in progress on the beach. It was fun to watch, but we were both glad we had the benefit of air-conditioning for some relief from our beach session.

I had been mulling over telling Gwen about the previous day's clandestine mission. Originally, I thought it best to wait until we recorded some concrete facts. But the more I thought about it, the more I felt like including her—regardless of her reaction. Before, I had apparently been more protective of Gwen than I needed to be.

More importantly, as close as we had become, I couldn't hold secrets from her anymore. It had only been maybe a month we had been together, but I had greater feelings for Gwen than any girl I had ever known. I had tried to convince myself that the stressful circumstances surrounding us might be influencing my infatuation toward her. But I was to the point where it didn't matter. I was a young adult, and my belief was I was old enough to decide that she was the one for me.

"Gwen," I said, "do you remember the night we were out this week, and I told you I had to go in to work on Saturday?"

"Sure."

"And do you also remember a little earlier when I told you that the guys and I would be trying to get some more information about the top brass at The Bank?"

"Yes," she said, "keep going."

"Well," I said, "there has been some major progress with our pursuit of said info. I did go to the complex yesterday, and so did Seth and Frankie. But it didn't have anything to do with our jobs."

"What do you mean?" she said.

"We now have a recording bug in Farr's office, and one in the conference room next door."

"You guys went in those offices?"

"No," I said, "we installed them from up in the attic area above each room. Frankie feels pretty confident he did it right."

"Wow," said Gwen, "it sure sounds risky. I think I am glad I didn't know about this before you did it. Getting caught would have been big trouble."

"Right," I said. "We had considered the possibilities."

With a little internal laugh, I thought to myself that maybe it was a good thing I hadn't told Gwen ahead of time. But more so, I felt better all around about being straight with her. I was continuing to realize Gwen was tougher on the inside than her overall demeanor would suggest. Maybe her New York fortitude was starting to show through. I knew deep down this was the time to let her know about the last piece of the puzzle.

"Gwen," I said, hesitating, "if things progress the way I think they might with all of this, I want you to know about a guy I met the night Tyler Morrison died. His name is Garth Milner."

"Hold on, Ben," said Gwen. "You've never told me how you actually know Tyler was killed. Were you there?"

"Yes…I was. I was a witness to his, uh, execution." I turned my head for a moment and looked out the window. After a slow breath, I turned back and said, "Remember you telling me about some possible upcoming activity at what you referred to as the Gator Lagoon? Well, that is where it happened…and that is where I met Garth. He was there because he believes his uncle met the same fate at the hands of The Bank. His uncle was a ranger at Ding Darling, and Garth thinks he got too nosy and was eliminated."

"You two just happened to bump into each other at night somewhere out in the refuge?" said Gwen.

"Let's put it this way," I said, "Garth helped me get out of there. He is a good guy. We rode on his boat back to his house in St. James City. Garth is a contractor with the Florida Fish and Wildlife Conservation Commission. Seth and Frankie have met him, too. It was on that Sunday when I told you we were making a road trip to Pine Island."

"Any other little tidbits I don't know about?"

"One more to go," I said. "The day we went over and met up with Garth, he introduced us to Katy Monroe. She is a reporter for the News-Press. Katy had done a profile article about Garth some time ago for another paper, and they have since become casual friends. Now she is doing more investigative reporting. Garth insisted on telling her about what went on that night. She wants to help us bust everything wide open, but we have to get better information first."

"What did go on that night?" asked Gwen.

"They call it the Gator Lagoon for a reason," I said. "Let's leave it at that."

"This is way more gruesome than I would ever imagine," she said.

"Right," I said. Then looking her straight in the eyes, "Look, Gwen, I've held some things back from you...for what I thought were good reasons. If I didn't care about you the way I do, maybe I would have told you some or all of this stuff earlier. I didn't want to hurt you...in any way."

Gwen rose up out of her chair, leaned across our table for two, and planted a firm kiss on my lips. She sat back down, took a sip of her wine and said, "So, what happens next?"

My feelings for Gwen soared over the top. I toasted her with my beer, smiled and said, "The recording system Frankie has set up at our house is voice activated. We are not expecting to get anything until tomorrow. Frankie is going to type out a transcript of conversations so we can read through them."

"It sounds like the escapade is heating up," she said.

"It was heated up yesterday, that's for sure," I said. "The temperature up above those offices was amazing. Frankie and I were a couple of wet noodles. It affected me, but it really took the wind out of Frankie's sails."

"And what was Seth's role?" she asked.

"Basically," I said, "he distracted the guard by taking him out of the building to show him his fishing reel. Seth can be quite the bullshitter. But he sure helped with his part of it."

"Let me know if you come up with anything on the recordings. I'm going to see if I can somehow capture any of the financial transfer data in my office."

"Look, Gwen," I said, "don't be taking any crazy chances with any of this. Like you just told me, it is big trouble to be getting into if anything goes wrong."

"Aye, Aye, Captain. What is that saying, 'discretion is the better part of valor'?"

"I think we all should be reminding each other of that one."

We enjoyed a nice lunch of grouper sandwiches, and then relaxed for a while viewing the scene on the beach with the azure waters of the Gulf of Mexico serving as the backdrop. I suggested we go back to my house for the balance of the afternoon. It was something we hadn't done. Gwen had not officially met the guys, and only recognized them in passing once or twice in the dining area of The Bank. But I figured Gwen, the guys, and I were now on the same squad.

"Sure," she said, "why not?"

We drove back to Gwen's car, and as I was dropping her off, the sky was taking on the common summer afternoon color of an impending thunderstorm. As Gwen followed me up Sanibel-Captiva Road, the darkening increased at a rapid pace. With about a mile to go, raindrops the size of silver dollars started splattering on the windshield. By the time I pulled into our gravel driveway off Dinkins Lake Road, visibility from the pounding rain was practically zero. I could see well enough to notice both of the guys' vehicles were out. A second after Gwen pulled in behind me, my cell phone rang.

"I am thinking," she said, "I shouldn't leave my car parked here in plain sight from the road. Any ideas?"

"Just pull around that big bougainvillea bush at the side of the house," I said, "and park behind it on the grass. I'll grab one of the beach towels for cover and I'll come and get you."

I pulled out a beach towel from the back seat and waited until her car was stopped. After a sprint to Gwen's car, she got out and we held the towel over our heads for a shield. The beach towel worked well as an umbrella for about twenty feet until Gwen lost her grip on it from a strong wind gust. As a result, we were soaked through from the relentless rainfall before we made it to the front porch. It had been a short distance to run, but a few seconds in an intense summer storm is all it takes around here to become completely drenched.

When we went inside it was confirmed that neither of the guys were home. I led Gwen up to my room and we proceeded to peel off our soaked clothes. That process led to an extended intimate rendezvous. The fierce thunderstorm added extra excitement to our passion, which was not diminished when the rain eventually stopped.

Several hours later, and after I had briefly tossed our wet clothing in the dryer, we dressed and came downstairs. Frankie was on one of the sofas watching a car race on television.

"Frankie," I said, "I'd like to introduce you to Gwen."

Frankie stood and shook Gwen's hand, saying, "Nice to meet you Gwen. I have seen you at The Bank a couple of times."

"Nice meeting you," said Gwen, smiling. "Now it is official."

"What have you been doing today?" I asked

Frankie.

"I was up in Fort Myers," he said, "helping a friend of mine who I know from back at Edison College. We did a brake job on his car. It was no big deal. But this guy can always come up with a few extra checklist items for me to fix whenever I give him a hand. Today it included putting up a ceiling fan, and cleaning up some junk on his old desktop computer."

I turned to Gwen and said, "He is a jack-of-all-trades."

"So they say," said Frankie.

She laughed and said to Frankie, "Seems like you are a good person to know."

We exchanged small talk chatter for a while until I brought up the subject we all had in common. "Frankie," I said, "I told Gwen about our project yesterday at the administration building. So she is up to date on everything that is going on. I've told her everything that has happened, Frankie. Everything."

"This is a good thing," said Frankie. "We can certainly use any help we can get."

"I am going to see if I can retrieve any information from the computer system," said Gwen.

"I worked in that department for a while," said Frankie. "You will have to be very careful with all of that."

"I know," she said. "My uncle is the boss of the department."

"Sorry," said Frankie, "it is just that we are all wandering into hazardous duty here. Avoiding trouble is key."

"I think we are all a little edgy," I said. "Let's face it, this is risky. But even if we don't get caught, we are all most likely out of jobs if we bring the big shots down. That, however, is a subject for another time. Anyway, Frankie, when you get any good info on the recorder, Gwen would like to meet with us to go over it."

"Fine," said Frankie, "Another set of ears could help. Let me have tomorrow night to practice transcribing the conversations we get on the recorder. Then we can have a meeting here Tuesday evening and, hopefully, we should have something interesting to go over from the two days."

"I'll be here," she said.

Gwen had to be getting back to her uncle's house for a dinner with neighbors. I walked her to her car, which was hiding comfortably behind the shrubbery. I encouraged Gwen to try to keep as calm and abstract as possible with her relatives considering the circumstances she was now facing. It had to be a grating situation to be in. But she seemed firmly resolved to press on.

Seth rolled in later and was somewhat of a mess. He had gone out fishing on a friend's boat from the marina at South Seas Plantation, which is at the north end of Captiva. Seth said they had almost made it back in before the earlier storm caught them. He said they got very soaked. So they proceeded to dry off for a few hours just down the road in the bar at the Mucky Duck. He said it was a wild show to watch the lightning dance on the Gulf.

Seth was still cognizant enough after the

drinking session to be filled in on Gwen's new involvement in our project. Like Frankie, Seth gave his own thumbs up to the newest member of our team. Even though he had never met Gwen, he said he was confident it was a sound decision on my part. If she was fine with me, he was fine with her.

So our meeting was set. It occurred to me to contact Garth, but I decided we should do the dry run with the transcripts before taking that step. I valued Garth's input, but I thought it best to wait until we had something we could go on. Now, if we can only get something tangible, I thought.

15

On Tuesday evening around seven, Gwen arrived at the house and we all gathered in the living room. Since they had missed each other on Sunday, I introduced Gwen to Seth. After they exchanged courteous greetings, we proceeded with the business at hand. Seth marked his territory by stretching full out on one of the sofas. Gwen and I took a seat on the other. Frankie sat upright on one of the easy chairs and called the meeting to order.

He had the voice recorder hooked up on the end table next to him, and gave each of us printed and stapled copies of the transcript. I was always impressed with Frankie's technical talents in a wide variety of areas, but he seemed to be taking on an even more intense approach with this project. He was displaying a certain enthusiasm I had never seen before.

"Okay," said Frankie, "I have gone through the tapes that were recorded in either Farr's office or the conference room from yesterday and today. It was very limited yesterday. I think Farr must have been out of his office in the afternoon. But today there were a couple of meetings.

"I printed up what I thought were the most interesting conversations. Both of the separate receivers we planted capture voices on the recorder so we can't know what was said in which room. It doesn't make any difference anyway. On your sheets there, we can all read along with the transcript. I indicated who I think was talking in each case. When we get to quotes where I wasn't sure who it was, I can skip forward on the recorder here so we can actually listen to the voices. But I guess that doesn't make much difference either. Alright, let's start. The first one has Farr, Ava Branstein, and Webb Dunn."

Farr: I've gotten word from our representatives in London that there could be trouble on the horizon for us. As you know, there have been several investigations over the past few years regarding manipulation of the LIBOR. Other world banks have received heavy fines for their transgressions in that area.

Dunn: Right, sir.

Branstein: Yes, sir.

Farr: Even though The Bank does not have the same amount of financial resources in the international banking industry, we are nonetheless subject to the same type of scrutiny from the regulators. Our resources, after all, substantial. McMillan in our London office has caught wind of an impending investigation of our practices. For quite some time, several of our traders have been, shall I say, rigging the daily interest rate submitted to LIBOR. This investigation could quite possibly go on to reveal the source of our main revenue supply.

Branstein: Sanchez.

Farr: Precisely. Although that would be a devastating development, it will not happen. We have established a brotherhood here with the Fraternal Members, which will not be overcome. We have built a strong presence in the banking world. There is a global agenda awaiting us for even greater wealth and authority. And our mantra of 'WAIN' remands strong.

Dunn: Yes, sir. Whatever action is necessary. I am prepared to impose any and all necessary acts to ensure that The Bank prevails.

      Frankie interrupted, "I didn't know how to spell 'WAIN' when I was typing it, but then realized it was an acronym when Dunn said, 'Whatever action is necessary.' And I capitalized LIBOR because

I know it is an acronym, too. It stands for London inter-bank offered rate. Is everyone okay so far?"

Gwen turned to me, saying, "Now we know what WAIN means. It was on the note on Uncle Harris' desk about the event at the Gator Lagoon."

"Are these people on a power trip, or what?" said Seth.

"Yeah," said Frankie, "that is what I was thinking. Let's keep reading."

Farr: I am calling a meeting of the Fraternal Members at two this afternoon. As usual for these confidential issues, the meeting will not be comprised of all our department heads. Operational managers will be excluded. However, I wanted to discuss this matter with both of you beforehand, so you would be prepared. That is all for now.

Dunn: Fine, sir.

Branstein: Very good, sir.

"Well," I said, looking at the guys, "it's nice to know none of our fathers are part of the Fraternal Members."

"Unfortunately," said Gwen, "my uncle will be right in the middle of what is going on, I'm sure."

"What's with this Fraternal Members crap?" said Seth.

"To me," said Frankie, "they are some kind of smaller version of other secret organizations. Like the Bohemian Grove group or the Freemasons, for example. Only, in this case, these guys are breaking all kinds of laws to go along with the secrecy. I mean, it is one thing to be secret, but it's a whole different story to be laundering drug money and to be killing people, to boot."

"How about that," said Seth, "Fraternal Members and Freemasons. F and M for both of them."

"And there was a symbol of the sun," I said, "the night at the Gator Lagoon. Plus, there was the same sun symbol on the pages of notes from Farr's office when I took the pictures. That is just coming back to me now. Hold on a second, everybody. I'm checking the pictures on my phone to find those notes. Here they are. Okay, some of the terms are *international agenda, fresh global disposition, secret oath, interest rate manipulation,* and *worldwide control.* And there is *WAIN* in all caps."

"These folks are going for the gusto," said Seth.

With a serious look, Gwen said. "Right. And we have to do what we can to help stop this runaway train."

"It sounds like The Bank is coming under fire from the international regulators," said Frankie. "But they may be slick enough to figure out a way to beat getting caught."

"The problem," I said, "is it's not just the interest rigging issue, or even the drug money. They are murderers, plain and simple. And we are the only people, besides Garth and Katy Monroe, who know it. We just can't prove it."

"I would say these transcripts could help," said Frankie.

"Yeah," I said, "for everything but the murders. The banking regulators, if they go after them, will just be scratching the surface on how bad these people are."

"Okay," said Frankie, "let's keep going. This next segment is the meeting at two today. I think I have identified most of the people talking. But bear in mind, if someone was in this meeting and didn't say anything; we don't know who they are."

Farr: With Ms. Branstein duly noted—Gentlemen, I have called this meeting to inform you all that there may well be an impending investigation into our company's financial dealings in London regarding the LIBOR. McMillan in the London office has reasonable knowledge to assume the international regulators will be looking into certain, uh, procedures our traders have taken. These procedures include manipulation of our offered interest rate to other world banks. If this investigation concludes we have indeed erred, I would imagine a hefty fine may well be levied against us. That being said, there may also be scrutiny into many of our other transactions. I want to be very clear in telling you we must take extra precautionary steps to include additional layers to our larger transactions that end up in our general account. This is in particular regard to funds generated from the A.I. account. As you all know, that account must always remain anonymous.

Multiple voices: Yes, sir.

Copeland: I will instruct the staff in my department to take such measures, sir. With the A.I. account, I will see to it that there are re-doubled efforts to weave extra transactions before the funds surface to the level of legitimacy.

Dunn: Rest assured, sir, that any misdeeds or shortcomings on the part of each and every single one of our employees will be met with the strictest of discipline.

Farr: Gentlemen, I believe we should proceed with cautious confidence in addressing this unfortunate matter. However, I also believe we will look back on this as a temporary inconvenience to our ultimate quest...domination of the financial world. We will become internationalists with no loyalty to any country. We will be The Bank of the World. It is our mission, and with the strength of our bond as Fraternal Members, we will not be deterred. We will continue to carry on in our pursuit of power and control. We are on a path that continues to trend upward...and there will be no leveling off. Complacency is destructive. And any setbacks will be dealt with accordingly. WAIN, Mr Dunn?"

Dunn: Whatever action is necessary, sir.

"So what do you think about that stuff?" said Frankie.

"Farr thinks he's freaking Hitler or something," said Seth.

"Wow," I said, "talk about scary."

"You know what strikes me about all this?"

said Gwen. "I really sense that Farr thinks he is doing the right thing. It is a trait of totalitarian leaders. They actually think they are doing the right thing."

"Well," I said, "for sure there is a wealth addiction going on."

"That is a nice term for greed," said Frankie.

"But they are blind to it," said Gwen. "And it's further ingrained in them by their motivation for the whole Fraternal Member thing. It is like they are gaining extra strength from each other...kind of like a gang mentality."

"This is a gang on steroids," said Seth. "Man, these dudes are something else."

"I bet some of them feel trapped," said Frankie.

"I don't know," I said, "by the time they have gotten to this inner group, I'd say they are all in with the agenda. It is more than just ambition. It is a rabid, fanatical drive to be number one. They don't even care if they are breaking laws to do it." I turned to Gwen and said, "It is a shame you have to go through this with your uncle involved."

Gwen didn't say anything, but tossed the palms of her hands up as if to say, "That's the way it is."

"I agree with you, Ben," said Frankie. "But as we have mentioned before, if this whole thing blows up and The Bank is history, our fathers, us, and other innocent people are out of work."

"The hell with them all," said Seth. "Everybody at The Bank is making way more money than they could anywhere else. All of our parents are loaded, and everybody is living the high life. This entire deal is screwed up, and I say we've got to stop it. I would just as soon be managing food and beverage at a restaurant or a country club than being involved with these assholes at the top."

"Now that you mention it," said Frankie, "if I ended up driving or getting a mechanic's job somewhere, it would be just fine with me."

"Look," I said, "all our dads and all of us are good enough at what we do to get another job in a heartbeat. None of us would be making as much money, but—."

"But," interrupted Gwen, "we wouldn't be working for a bunch of crooks and murderers, either."

"Let's toast to that," I said.

We all raised our cans of beer and clanked them together in a hearty toast. There were several moments of quiet that followed. Although we were all committed to a common goal, I think everyone was digesting the prospects of life after The Bank in their own way.

Frankie finally broke the silence, saying, "Come on, we have to finish up this last part of the transcript."

Farr: Due to the confidential nature of our meeting, and in view of our London branch's involvement, I have not included Mr. McMillan from that office in this meeting via conference call today. However, Mr. Covington, I know you have been listening in from the Andros branch.

Covington (voice distorted): Yes, sir.

Farr: I have seen the email with the latest financial data from your office. Beyond the numbers on the report, do you have any feel for the potential revenue flow into the Sanchez account over the next month?

Covington: Yes, sir. Only two days ago, their representative informed me that we should be expecting a massive deposit within the next two weeks. It will all be in U.S. currency.

Farr: Thank you, Mr. Covington. That is helpful information considering the difficulty in which we may find ourselves. Carry on with your good work, Fraternal Member.

Covington: Yes, sir.

"How 'bout that shit," said Seth. "Farr is keeping all the bases covered when it comes to the money."

"You bet," I said. "Sounds like he wants to have an exit strategy if everything hits the fan."

"Well," said Frankie, "There would be some kind of hell to pay if he tried to make off with Sanchez's cash. His people would catch up with Farr and the rest of them before the cops would."

"You know what?" said Gwen. "He doesn't think about a consequence like that. I am telling you, Farr and the others are sailing along on a different level. They think they're immune to everything."

"Indestructible," I said.

"That's what they think," said Gwen.

It occurred to me that a get-together with Garth and Katy Monroe was in order. I made a motion, which was seconded by all, to schedule a meeting with them on Sunday afternoon over in St. James City. In the back of my mind, I also quickly envisioned a weekend getaway with Gwen at Tarpon Lodge on the northern part of Pine Island. I was thinking we could stay there Friday and Saturday nights, and then drive the short distance to meet Seth and Frankie at Garth's house on Sunday. My mind was clicking.

I called Garth and he confirmed he was available on Sunday. Garth told me to tell the others he said to "bring it on." In the meantime he would contact Katy and let her know we were meeting at his house at two.

While Seth was in the bathroom and Frankie was in the kitchen, I floated a short version of my extra idea for the weekend past Gwen. She agreed it was an outstanding plan.

When the guys returned I told them Gwen and I would be seeing them at Garth's at two on Sunday. Frankie quickly chimed in that he would be driving Seth in his Camaro. I think Frankie knew right away he wanted to be in charge with his own car for the trip. That way he could dictate the departure time to come back home. When Frankie was driving us all in Seth's van for an outing, there were occasional times when Seth became difficult about leaving somewhere since it was his vehicle. Because it would just be one-on-one with Seth this time, I think Frankie wanted be sure he was avoiding a potentially uncomfortable situation.

So, all parties were set with the arrangements. I didn't know what the gathering would generate in the way of specific actions, but it was encouraging to hear Garth's raspy voice and his upbeat manner. Whether or not he could do anything to help us didn't really matter. His supportive attitude and confident approach to things helped bolster me. I knew there would be enjoyable times with Gwen on the weekend, and I was eagerly anticipating them. But, also, I was truly looking forward to seeing Garth on Sunday. He and his house seemed like a friendly port in a storm.

16

Friday evening Gwen and I met, as usual, to leave her car at the Olde Sanibel Shoppes parking lot. Even though it is a long drive to Pine Island from Sanibel, it was the weekend after Labor Day, so traffic was not bad. I would have enjoyed the time together with Gwen under any conditions.

We arrived at Tarpon Lodge around eight and checked into one of the cottages. It was a step up in size from the rooms in the historic lodge. Overall, the entire resort is an exclusive and expensive destination. The cottage we were staying in was separate and very private. Besides the bedroom, it had a living area and a dinette. Plus, it had a porch, which would have been useful in cooler months. It sure wasn't the case in the summertime. The air-conditioning was cranking away inside.

We got to the bar in the main building in need of some major food fortification. We made it in time to each get a massive cheeseburger that hit the spot. To enhance the atmosphere, a steel drum player was putting out relaxing island sounds. I had a momentary flashback to the solemn drummer the night at the Gator Lagoon, but I squelched it in a hurry. The vibes we were enjoying had the complete opposite effect on the listener compared to the woeful percussion I was remembering.

But I have to admit there had been occasional times when fleeting images of the events that night flashed through my mind. It was like I had taken still photographs of the proceedings and, for a second, one of the pictures jumped into my head. And it was always vivid. As the weeks had passed, the frequency of the flashbacks had lessened—but it was still something that haunted me. I was hoping for a healing effect with the passage of time. However, I knew there was very little chance the crystal-clear visual memories would ever disappear entirely.

After a cozy night of love and television viewing, we awoke to a blazing hot late-summer day. Since we had no specific plans for Saturday anyway, we enjoyed the day in the comfortable cottage. Everything about the accommodations was first-class. It was a relaxing relief from not only the day-to-day grind at The Bank, but also from the added stress we found ourselves under.

For dinner, we drove a short way down Stringfellow Road to Red's Fresh Seafood House. It was a touch more casual than the dining room at Tarpon Lodge, which made it more our style. We both made plenty of money, and could really afford to eat or stay most anywhere, but we each enjoyed less formalities. In our upbringings, Gwen and I had taken part in upscale events and pricey experiences, but we clicked when it came to more down-to-earth enjoyment. We each had found that having a good time didn't necessarily depend on how much money was spent.

We had an appetizer of Oysters Rockefeller, followed by two delicious grouper dinners. A bottle of Sauvignon Blanc was the perfect complement to the seafood dinner. For the most part during the weekend, we had avoided the issue of The Bank. But it was unrealistic to think it was a subject that could be neatly tucked away and left alone forever. After our meal, we relaxed and sipped on the rest of the bottle of wine. I could see a wave of seriousness starting to fall over Gwen.

"Uncle Harris," said Gwen, "has become increasingly gruff and surly at the house. It is especially noticeable when he has been drinking. There is a direct relationship between the level of his negative behavior and his intake of alcohol."

"It has to be an unpleasant situation for you," I said.

"He has started questioning me," she said, "about my personal activities and absences from the house in the evenings during the week and on weekends. I told him I was seeing a guy, and left it at that. Uncle Harris is starting to be even more of a control freak than before. There seems to be a correlation to the ramped up pressure in the office recently. I know my dad would not be happy to see the change in Uncle Harris. And I am sure it is not what my father had in mind when he encouraged me to move down here and take this job."

"I would imagine it is not what any parent would want," I said.

"But, Ben, it is making me even more motivated about what we are doing. Plus, when I see what all this blind ambition is doing to people in my office, it is really sickening. The demands from my uncle to produce, the backstabbing and the undermining of co-workers—it is changing people."

"How do you mean?" I asked.

"Well," said Gwen, "it is getting more intense all the time. People asking about the private lives of others. Always looking for some weakness to exploit for their own personal gain. And the highlighting of errors, if one is made, is a popular one. Anything that can be used to step on others to push them down and climb over them. It's always happening. The whole atmosphere is a turn-off for me. I really hope we can manage to do something to scuttle this evil ship."

We retired to our cottage at Tarpon Lodge, and coped with the flare-up of talk about The Bank by concentrating on each other. There was a continuing harmony between us, and it was capable of overriding the greater anxiety that hovered above. Here we were living in a part of the world that has been described as paradise, but Gwen and I were experiencing anything but the blissful peace of mind that paradise ought to create. Yet, our determination to rise above the challenges we were facing continued to increase.

On Sunday we checked out of the cottage and enjoyed a fine brunch in the dining room of Tarpon Lodge. On the drive down Stringfellow Road to Garth's house, I noticed Gwen digging through her oversized handbag, and rustling through some papers.

"Oh, Ben," she said, "I brought some information along. It may be helpful for the meeting today."

"What do you have there?"

"I just happen to have brought two sets of printouts from recent transactions in the A.I. account."

"What?"

"Yeah," said Gwen, "I stayed a little late after work on Thursday and ran them off."

"And this is the first you are telling me about this?"

"Well," she said, "you have been known to hold back certain information from time to time. I was just trying to be like you." Then with a wry smile, "And I also wanted to be like Farr. I wanted to tell you about this before the meeting so you would be, uh, prepared."

"Oh," I said, laughing. "Funny girl."

Just before two, we were the first to arrive at Garth's house. As we pulled up, Garth came out the door and greeted us on the front deck.

"Hey, hey, hey," came out of him in a gravely roar through a broad smile. He put a bear hug on me and said, "It's good to see you."

"Good to see you, Garth," I said. "I'd like you to meet Gwen. She works at The Bank, and is a good friend. Gwen is part of our group. She's the girl I mentioned to you the night we were coming back here from the refuge in your boat."

"Oh," he said, "right, right. I remember. Nice to meet you Miss Gwen."

"The feeling is mutual, Garth," said Gwen. "I've been looking forward to meeting you."

"Well, come on in," said Garth. "Let's get in the air-conditioning."

In a matter of minutes, Frankie and Seth arrived. When they came in, Garth hugged them both. Garth and Seth exchanged knowing grins. With a laugh, Garth said, "None of those vodka shots, chum."

Seth laughed and said, "Looks like you are safe today, Garth."

Garth had laid in plenty of beer, however. When he opened the refrigerator door to offer us one, half of the interior was lined with beer cans. Considering the environmentalist Garth was, I think he foresaw the potential for plenty of empty cans to put in the recycle. He could crush a large amount of cans to a smaller size, compared to the bottles he usually stocked.

We all toasted freshly opened beers, and in a short time Katy Monroe was at the front door. Once again she had on a peasant dress, which enhanced her overall flower child appearance. The girls were introduced and a brief period of socializing followed. After an appropriate amount of time, I got to the matter at hand.

"What do you say we sit at the kitchen table and go over what we have?"

Garth pulled several folding chairs out of the closet and the six of us assembled in snug fashion at the modestly-sized table.

"Garth and Katy," said Frankie, "for both of you, I've made extra copies of the transcripts."

Gwen spoke up, saying, "And I have printouts of transactions in the Andros Island account."

"That is great," said Frankie, "How did you pull that off, Gwen?"

"Let's just say," Gwen said with a laugh, "we each have our own specialized skills in this group."

"Seth exercised his skills," said Frankie, "when he bullshitted the guard while Ben and I were up in the thousand-degree attic bugging the offices."

"Good one, Frankie," said Seth.

Paperwork was shuffled around and pored over. Frankie and Gwen took turns explaining and highlighting various sections of the information they had supplied. After lengthy discussion, there was an abrupt and strange period of quiet among all of us.

I turned and looked straight at Katy, saying, "So what do you think?"

"Well, folks," she said, "this is all extremely

interesting. When you put this information we have been talking about together with the, um, executions, it is hard to believe. Connecting the dots, these bastards should either fry or at least go away for a long, long time. Based on what was said in the meetings, the head honchos are expecting an investigation on the insider trading."

"But that will just turn out to be a fine," said Frankie.

"Right," said Katy. "The drug money certainly ratchets things up. But they are doing this in the Bahamas where the government is known to turn a blind eye when it comes to banking. With all of these additional transactions, though, the international regulators could probably turn the screws and make The Bank explain them backwards until they got to the source of the money. What they are doing is like running a fencing operation. But instead of fencing stolen property and getting it back into what looks like a legitimate market, they are doing the same thing with cash."

"The definition of money laundering," said Gwen.

"Exactly," said Katy.

"I bet," said Seth, "just like in fencing stolen property, The Bank keeps a percentage of the cash."

"Yeah," said Frankie, "you deposit a million bucks of drug money and you get credit for depositing, I don't know, eight hundred thousand, or something like that."

"Wouldn't surprise me in the least," said Katy.

"But unfortunately," I said, "the murders are the only thing we don't have solid evidence of."

"Yeah," barked Garth, "no moving pictures with sound to capture the scene of somebody getting torn apart by a gang of alligators."

Gwen turned and shot a glance of disbelief at me, and then silently dropped her face into her hands. I had kept that gory detail from her for a reason. But it was only fitting that she now knew what the rest of us did. Garth had inadvertently completed the circle.

Gwen raised her head, and with a hardened look of determination said, "We have got to do whatever we can to stop them."

"Okay," said Katy, "for now, I'll take these transcripts and the printouts of the transactions and compile them into a mock draft of an article. Don't know about adding in the gator issue just yet."

"Without any proof, Miss Katy," said Garth, "that would most likely get you into some deep do-do."

"Or worse," I said. "I think the best plan is to keep gathering information from the office recordings to see if we can pick up any inkling of some move they are planning to make."

"Agreed," said Katy. "Something else might tip the scales to the point where it becomes more than just a financial investigation. Something with a little more meat to it."

"Excuse the comparison, and not to be gruesome," said Garth, "but let's hope that somebody else doesn't have to end up in bits and pieces in the Gator Lagoon for that to happen."

"If we can get something concrete," said Katy, "I will get in touch with the Assistant Police Chief on Sanibel I had mentioned before. We were good friends way back when we were at Cypress Lake High School in Fort Myers. We still run into each other every now and then. This mess is taking place in his jurisdiction after all."

Around four-thiry, Katy had to leave so we wrapped up the meeting. There had been such intensity while we all were sitting there that the beer intake was very limited. I would guess no one had more than two. No one except Seth, of course. He had been subtle in helping himself to at least five or six reinforcements from the refrigerator during the course of our discussion. So really, it meant Seth had been light with the drinking, too. No one overdid things, which was good. Also, Garth was left with a big inventory of beer to work on for a while.

The four of us said our goodbyes to Garth, which included a gentle handshake with Gwen and almost bone-crushing hugs with Seth, Frankie, and me. Garth had a way of making you feel better because of the way he felt about you. It was a positive sentiment all the way around.

As Gwen and I followed Frankie's Camaro home, we had music on the radio and talked very little. During the drive, I looked at lush vegetation the summer rains bring, looked at the brilliant blue sky dotted with pure-white puffy clouds, and stole momentary looks at Gwen. I had difficulty believing it was all such a contradiction with what else was happening in our lives. Off and on, Gwen put her hand on my shoulder and clutched it with a reassuring grip. We are in this, I thought. We have to see it through.

17

Frankie kept tabs on the recordings from Farr's office and the conference room over the course of the week, but nothing of particular interest was generated. However, when Frankie got back to the house after work on Thursday, a red flag was run up the pole. He told Seth and me he was calling a short-notice meeting at seven-thirty, and that he would be busy until then typing up transcripts.

I called Gwen right away and she told me she would be over to the house in time for the meeting. What would normally have been a standard Thursday night for the three guys to go out had been turned into our own version of a hurry-up domestic pow-wow.

I drove down to the Sanibel Deli on Palm Ridge Road and picked up sandwiches for the four of us. As was his nature, Seth made a run to pick up a supply of beer. I got back to the house just as Gwen was pulling into her personal parking spot behind the enormous bougainvillea bush.

A few minutes before seven-thirty, Frankie came downstairs with the voice recorder and a stack of papers in his hands. There was a serious look on his face as he set the recorder down on the end table. Frankie took a seat and passed out the sheets.

"Lady and gentlemen," said Frankie, "I believe we have captured some compelling information on the tape today."

"What?" said Seth. "Did Farr fart when nobody else was in the office and you have it on tape?"

"Very funny," Frankie deadpanned. "Not quite that. But let's read through what did happen during a hastily-called meeting this afternoon. I typed it up like before."

Farr: Ms. Branstein and gentlemen, I have called this meeting for several reasons. First, I have received information indicating The Bank will, indeed, be the subject of an investigation by the international regulators. This is a serious matter but, in and of itself, not as troubling as perhaps where things may lead. As I have directed you before, safeguards concerning transactions from the A.I. account are paramount.

Multiple voices: Yes, sir.

Farr: Fraternal Members, we are as one. The bond of our brotherhood in reaching our common goal is what sustains us. We will not be denied that goal. Nothing will stand in our way. Unfortunately, a severe shortcoming in the proper implementation of our secure procedures has been uncovered. Therefore, I am calling a cleansing assembly at the Gator Lagoon tomorrow evening. You will all report promptly to the parking area at nine-o'clock for the ceremonial procession. The pathway will be prepared. Be attired in formal regalia.

Multiple voices: Yes, sir.

Farr (voice rising): Fraternal Members, we are a power elite. And our secretive nature makes our union supremely strong. There cannot be any cracks in our armor. There will be no breach which holds us short of our destiny. We are the Fraternal Members and we will triumph. Control of the world banking system is within our reach. We have the potential to achieve victory and we will not be denied.

Multiple voices (high volume): Yes, sir.

Seth interrupted and said, "Well isn't that a hoot. I bet there were some sphincters tightening up in the conference room during this."

"No kidding," I said. "Wow, a 'cleansing assembly.' Well isn't that a wonderful masquerade of a term. I wonder who the next victim will be."

"You know," said Seth, "I've done enough fishing to make this comparison. Farr and The Bank are like bonefish. They are tough fighters, they're ruthless, and they have these primitive instincts. They are freaking bonefish."

"We have to be there, Ben," said Frankie, "And, we have to film it."

"Hold on a minute, Frankie," I said. "I'm going to call Garth. Let's get his take on this."

As I scrolled down on my cell phone for Garth's number, I caught a fleeting glance of Gwen. She looked more stern than worried.

"Garth," I said, "it's Ben. From the tapes today, we know that the higher powers at The Bank are going to have another gathering at the Gator Lagoon tomorrow night."

"Is that right?" said Garth, more like a statement than a question.

"Yes," I said. "They are referring to it as a 'cleansing assembly,' if you can believe that. The guys and Gwen and I are all here together going over the transcript, and there has been some talk among us of going and filming it. What do you think? Should we call the police? Hold on a second, Garth. I'm going to put you on speaker phone so we all can hear."

"Hey there, chums," said Garth in his raspy voice, "and you too, Gwen."

"Hi, Garth," they all chimed in.

"Wow," he said, "you are catching me a little off guard, but let's see here. No, I don't think calling the cops is such a good idea. I mean, what are you going to tell them? It would take a mess of explaining, and none of it would sound possible. They would think you were suggesting they go trudging out at night in the middle of Ding Darling to stop some secret execution. It would probably be looked on by them like some kind of wild goose chase. You know, like kids do for fun at summer camp."

"I don't know, Garth," I said, "we have to do something. We don't have the firepower or the inclination to go in there and take them on to try to stop it."

"I agree with you there, chum," said Garth. "Okay, here is what I suggest. Ben, you get yourself over here to my place after you're done work tomorrow. We'll take my boat and kayak and go into the refuge the same way we came back together the other time."

"Garth," said Frankie, "I really would like to be in on this. I could do the filming. I have a great little video recorder."

"I don't think so, Frankie," said Garth. "My double kayak is only built for two passengers, and it would make another set of footsteps once we got on dry land."

I saw that Frankie had a pleading look on his face. "How about it, Garth?" I said. "Frankie is really good with the technical stuff. And it would be another set of eyes and ears. Plus, as you know, he is not a big guy."

"Yeah," said Seth, "just slightly bigger than a horse racing jockey. And younger looking."

"Well," said Garth. "I guess it would be alright, Ben. But he will have to straddle over the top of the kayak behind your back in the cat bird's seat."

"That is fine with me," said Frankie.

"Okay," said Garth, "I'm going to let Katy Monroe know about this, but no matter how much she hounds me to go with us, and I know she will, I'm not letting her come along. Nor would I allow you, Miss Gwen. I am not a sexist in the least, but this is pretty rough stuff. And that big galoot, Seth, would never get his big ol' bod through those mangroves anyway. Besides, Ben and I have done it once before. We've got experience."

"That we do, Garth," I said. "Tomorrow night the participants are meeting at nine to start the procession to the Gator Lagoon. And they will, once again, be dolled up in their colorful robes. From what we have been reading along on here, they must create a path though the mangroves to get to the lagoon. And I bet by the next morning the path doesn't exist anymore."

"You guys get over here tomorrow evening as soon as you're able," said Garth. "Then we'll make our way over there and get set up. I don't want to see somebody else get killed, none of us do. But if we get this recorded, I think we've got them."

"We will be there, Garth," I said.

"And for both of you, long pants and long sleeves."

"Got it, Garth," said Frankie.

I ended the phone call and it was followed by several minutes of silence. Gwen put her hand on my knee and gave it a firm clutch. Frankie squirmed a bit in his seat with nervous excitement.

Finally, Seth said, "You guys can do it. You're going to have Garth with you. You can do it."

The meeting broke up and Gwen and I lingered on the sofa. Seth and Frankie grabbed their sandwiches out of the refrigerator. When they returned with them and turned on the television,

Gwen and I moved to the kitchen table and proceeded to pick over our sandwiches in silence. Both of us had lost our appetite.

After I wrapped up our plentiful leftovers and put them in the refrigerator, Gwen and I decided to withdraw to my room. As we passed through the living room, each of the guys stood up and took turns hugging both me and Gwen. It was an uplifting feeling. As Seth and I broke apart, he said, "You are both going to do fine tomorrow night. I know it."

"Thanks," I said, "we're going to give it the old college try."

When Gwen and I got into my room, she turned off the light and, in essence, tackled me down onto the bed. She buried her head into my shoulder and held me tighter than I could remember. After only a few moments, I could tell she was crying.

She lifted her head and, in the near-darkness, I could see tears running down her cheeks. "Oh, Ben, this is awful," she said. "I know what you are going to do can help solve all this, but I don't want to see anything happen to you."

"Look, Gwen," I said, "We all want to see this through. I agree with Garth. None of us want somebody else to get killed, but doing this might be the clincher to end the madness that has been going on."

"Oh, Ben," she said, "I am so worried, I don't know what to do. I guess I am supposed to just sit around tomorrow night fretting about how you are."

"I will call you on your cell phone," I said,

"as soon as we get back to Garth's house. It's going to work out fine. Garth is the man to be with. He knows what he is doing. And you know Frankie is the techno guy. I am in good hands. Do you think you will be staying home tomorrow evening?"

"Yeah," said Gwen, "without a doubt, I will be barricaded in my personal section of my uncle's house. That is basically what my life has become there." After a short pause, and with a smirk, she said, "Of course, I probably don't have to worry about Uncle Harris being around tomorrow night. He has a meeting at the Gator Lagoon."

"Yes," I said, "I guess he sure does."

Gwen went on, "Uncle Harris continues to be more on edge as every day goes by. He has these flare-ups with my aunt, and he keeps questioning me about my goings-on. I really think he is losing it. I feel like I've been walking on eggs around there, and I am not sure how much longer I can take it."

"When we get this video," I said, "it will soon be coming to an end."

Gwen put her head back deep into my shoulder and held me even tighter. There was the slightest trembling through her body. I pulled back and kissed her hard, and she returned it in kind.

"I love you," I said.

"I love you, too" said Gwen.

We went on to love each other with passion like never before. We were energized in our expression of affection.

It was just after eleven when we went downstairs. Frankie had apparently gone to bed, and Seth was sprawled out on one of the sofas in a deep sleep. I went out with Gwen and we walked around the house to her car in bright moonlight. The sole issue putting a huge damper on an unhurried goodbye was a swarm of mosquitoes doing double duty in their attack of us. I told Gwen I would call her right after I got off from work, before Frankie and I left for Garth's.

On the scramble back to the safety of the house, I caught a glimpse of what was an otherwise beautiful summer night. Although the standard stickiness of humidity was in the air, there was a gentle breeze and there was not a cloud in the sky. The mosquitoes had done a good job of taking the edge off the atmosphere of the pleasant night. But in terms of a hassling tension, it was the anticipation of what the next evening would bring that beat the mosquitoes by a mile.

18

Friday dragged on like it was in slow motion. When the workday finally ended I could hardly remember what projects I had been involved in handling. I called Gwen's cell phone but got her voice mail. She may have been working a little late, so I left her a message telling her I would call back before Frankie and I started off to Garth's house.

Frankie was delayed at work and got to the house about forty-five minutes after I did. It was too hot to travel to Garth's place in anything but shorts and a tank top, so I packed a duffle bag with a long sleeve shirt, long pants, and another change of clothes including shorts and a T-shirt. In the back of my mind I thought there was a good chance Frankie and I would be spending the night at Garth's house. Even though Frankie got home after me, he was quickly ready to go. He had planned ahead of time by packing a bag the night before.

I called Gwen again. It was a brief conversation that basically consisted of her telling me over and over again to be careful. What was easier said than done was me telling her not to worry. I told her I would call when we returned to Garth's house after the secretive mission.

I had volunteered to drive, so we loaded everything into my Jeep and headed out. We stopped at Bailey's for sandwiches, various snacks, and a case of spring water. It was far better preparation than my first sortie to the Gator Lagoon. The groundwork for that trip was non-existent.

When we arrived at Garth's, he greeted each of us with a pat on the back and a growling, "Good to see you, chums."

There was impatience in the air as we sat in his house for a brief twenty minutes that seemed like hours. A little before eight, Garth said we should be leaving so we could make the hike to the Gator Lagoon while there was still some light in the sky. Frankie and I each did a quick change into our long sleeves and long pants before we shoved off from Garth's dock.

After we crossed Pine Island Sound, Garth guided his boat into the mangroves on the back side of Ding Darling. He brought us to the same hidden spot under hanging seagrapes and mangroves as the time before. With cautious care, the three of us transitioned to the two-seat kayak. Frankie did as Garth instructed and straddled between the front and back seat. When we were all aboard and tucked together, it seemed as if we were teammates in a bobsled.

Frankie kept his hands on the back of my shoulders as Garth and I paddled us along. Just as the night Garth rescued me, he was the one providing the stronger stroke of the oar and the steady hand of the navigator.

We came to a stop at a point where the slow-moving tributary narrowed. It could well have been the same location he had hidden the kayak the previous time. But that particular night it was close to darkness and I had definitely not been thinking with a clear head.

We stepped out into ankle-deep water and helped Garth slide the kayak into the underbrush. Garth took out a hunting knife and cut off three mangrove branches that he laid as cover over the kayak.

Leading the way, Garth strode ahead of Frankie as I took up the rear in our single-file march through the crooked maze of mangroves. The two positives compared to our escape on the first occasion were there was some light in the sky, and the pace was less frantic.

We arrived at the edge of the clearing where the low stage was set up. There was no breeze and heavy evening humidity hung in the air. Combining those discomforts with our trek through the mangroves, the three of us were all soaked in sweat. And with the diminishing light, the first of the mosquitoes began their assault on us.

The only people in sight were several security guards milling around, and the lone blue-robed drummer to the left of the podium. We each spread apart several feet and, with a great effort to be quiet, took positions lending a view of the assembly area. As Frankie was looking over his small video recorder, I tapped him on the arm and motioned to the low-lying pond beyond and to the side of the stage. In the fading light, we could see six or seven alligators lying still, both in and near the water.

A security guard made the circuit around the clearing to light the array of spiked torches. As he walked the perimeter, he passed within no more than ten or twelve feet of us. Although Garth, Frankie, and I were motionless and quiet, I felt like the heavy pounding of my heart could be heard for miles. It was a sure bet the same was true for the other guys.

When the torches were all lit, the drummer began the slow beat of a recurring, cadenced riff. It was an all too familiar sound, and one I had hoped I would never hear again. As before, the illumination of the flames cast a flickering glow on the sun symbol above the stage.

It was an anxious situation for me and for Garth, but we had experienced it before. Considering Frankie's nervous energy and lack of familiarity with the scene, I imagined he was coming out of his skin. He busied himself by taking a panoramic video of the surrounding area. Since the recorder looked very upscale, it most likely had an anti-shake feature. That was a good thing since I could see from the light of the torches that Frankie was having trouble holding the camera steady.

In about ten minutes, the balance of the security detail arrived with Webb Dunn in their company. All of the guards assumed a position of attention as a procession of a half- dozen brightly-robed executives emerged from an opening on the opposite side of the clearing from us. Lucien Farr, who was leading, stepped to the stage as the others lined up in the opening and faced him. Ava Branstein and Harris Copeland were among the group of high-level managers. When Farr reached the podium, the drumming stopped.

"Fraternal Members," said Farr, "it is with great disappointment we must assemble once again here at the Gator Lagoon. But it is a necessity, which is required when the security of The Bank is at risk."

I shot a glance at Frankie to see him filming away as Farr continued, "Regrettably, we have been confronted with an inadequacy in the performance of

170

transactions regarding our most crucial account. As you know, our Security Director, Mr. Dunn has made it crystal-clear that such failings will not be tolerated. Therefore, we will proceed to administer appropriate punishment."

Farr turned and motioned toward the security detail, bellowing, "I give you, Evan Montgomery."

Forgetting he was still filming, Frankie made an abrupt turn to me and choked out in a whisper, "I know Evan from working in the department. Tell me this is not happening."

Frankie got himself together and aimed the video recorder back in the proper direction as Evan Montgomery was led forward to a spot in front of Farr. Montgomery's hands were secured behind his back with plastic ties. But the two differences I noticed from the first ceremony were that he already had duct tape over his mouth, and he was not blind-folded. I started to have eerie flashbacks to the same images I'd had recurring visions of since the first sickening occurrence. I shook my head to clear it, and could feel sweat flying off my face.

"Mr. Montgomery," boomed Farr, "transgressions of underperformance such as those you have committed will not be tolerated at The Bank." Then motioning back and to the side, Farr said, "You must pay the price, sir."

As Evan Montgomery was dragged, struggling, toward the pond, the lights around its perimeter were switched on. It was a horrible replay of the same course of action Garth and I had witnessed before. I could see Frankie was having some trouble keeping still, so I gave him a reassuring grip on his shoulder. He was startled by the contact and lurched around toward me. He turned back and aimed the video recorder in time to film the tie wraps on Montgomery's hands being cut off, and the duct tape being stripped from his mouth by the guards.

"No," screamed Montgomery as he was manhandled and thrust into the Gator Lagoon. The alligators quickly descended on their prey. As the first time, fierce thrashing followed. The flurry quickly settled down to only an occasional splash of an alligator tail.

I turned toward Garth to see him motioning his head as if to suggest we should leave. Frankie, who was between us, turned and doubled over with several dry heaves. He kept a grip on the recorder, but with his free hand he caught onto a branch and snapped it with a sharp crack, losing his balance and falling to the ground. As I grabbed for Frankie, I saw the heads of the assembled group turn in our direction. At once, the squad of security guards on the other side of the clearing broke into a sprint toward us.

I hoisted Frankie up by his waist and pushed him in Garth's direction. I followed the two of them as Garth led the way in a hasty retreat. As the first time Garth and I had done this very thing, a near-full moon provided some light for our escape. One advantage we had over the guards tracking us was that we had a good idea of our route, while they would have to scatter in various directions.

Frankie was doing a good job of keeping up with Garth, and I was not far behind when I tripped on a mangrove root and fell face first to the ground. As I was just to my knees and hurrying to get up, I was slammed back down to the ground from behind. A forearm bore down on my neck, and I felt what seemed to be a gun barrel pressed hard on the back of my head.

"You stay still right there while I radio in," said a man's stern voice.

Before he said another word, I felt the end of the gun barrel knocked away from my head and the security guard's body rolled off of me. I hadn't yet turned over when I heard a gross crunching sound. As I sat up, Garth grabbed me by the arm and pulled me to my feet. In the moonlight, I could see the guard's motionless body slumped in a heap on the ground.

"Let's get the hell out of here, chum," said Garth.

Frankie was waiting for us a short distance away as we started up our withdrawal once again. Garth took the lead and set a pace that Frankie and I tracked. Adrenalin was on overload as we pressed on through the maze of mangroves.

We got to the kayak and were pulling the branches off of it when several shots were fired in our direction. In short order, we piled in and pushed off. We managed to get around a bend in the tributary and out of our pursuers' line of sight.

When we got to the canopy of mangroves where Garth's fishing boat was hidden, I had to pry Frankie's hands out of the vise grip he had on my shoulders. Through it all, Frankie had the video recorder well secured with a strap around his neck. We boarded the boat and Garth tied down the kayak.

On the way back across Pine Island Sound to St. James City, none of us said a word. But there were a few glances back and forth among us that spoke for themselves. The breeze flowing over us as we cruised ahead at full throttle was helpful to mind and body. It was a refreshing change.

When we got to the dock behind Garth's house, he guided the boat to a flawless stop. After securing it, we shuffled our way inside.

"Well, chums," said Garth, "that was some kind of interesting evening. You two okay? I say we have a beer."

Frankie and I felt ourselves over only to find a few minor scrapes and scratches. I went into the bathroom to look at my nose, which had been throbbing. There was no bleeding, but I had a strawberry abrasion on it from when I had been slammed down on the ground. It was going to be a nice item to explain to Gwen. Plus, the way my nose and face hurt in general, I anticipated a black eye or two would be appearing in a day or so.

The reality of what had happened, or what could have happened was sinking in, and it wasn't a pleasant feeling. If it hadn't been for Garth...I didn't want to think about it.

Garth turned the radio on with his classical music station playing. The three of us gathered at the kitchen table and opened beers he brought from the refrigerator.

"We did it, chums," Garth said as we toasted.

"Garth," I said, "what you did back there, well, you saved my life."

"Yeah," said Garth, "I learned that little maneuver back in the day when I was in the Navy SEALs. Don't believe I've told you chums about those days. I don't really like to think about it anymore. Look, when you are growing up you're taught to be nice to people, and not to hurt people. Then, in the service they teach you the complete opposite. It messes with your head. Unfortunately, there can come a time when it is a matter of kill or be killed, like tonight. Not something I want to make a habit of, though."

After a few minutes of fiddling with the recorder, Frankie said, "Okay, I looked it over, and we have the video and probably the sound, too. But if it is alright with you guys, I would just as soon wait until tomorrow to watch the whole thing over with the audio. In the meantime, I'm going to hook up the recorder to your laptop and save it there, Garth. I also brought along three memory sticks I'll transfer it onto."

"That is one fancy piece of equipment, chum," said Garth.

"It's a GoPro camera," said Frankie. "They have only been making them for a couple of years. This one doesn't have as many features as the more expensive ones. But it has good sound recording and good stabilization when it is moved around, or when you are filming action."

"All of those were nice features to have tonight," I said.

"Yeah," said Frankie, "sorry about losing it there a couple of times while I was filming." Then after hesitating, "I knew Evan Montgomery from my time in Data Processing. I liked him. He was a nice guy. I couldn't believe what was happening to him."

"You did fine," said Garth. "Ben here, and I had been through it once before. And it's not something any of us are planning to do again. You did just fine."

We decided there had to be a meeting of our whole group to watch, and distribute, the video. We settled on eleven the next morning, and each of us made a phone call. Garth called Katy Monroe, Frankie called Seth, and I called Gwen.

After several repeated assurances to Gwen that everything went okay, she confirmed she would meet Seth at the house in the morning between nine and nine-thirty. I told her if she couldn't get any answer at the door, to just honk the heck out of her car horn until Seth came out. It would be a surefire way to rouse him since Gwen parked her car beside the house directly below Seth's bedroom window.

Frankie set things up with Seth to drive Gwen in his van. I could make out in the mixed blur of multiple phone conversations that Frankie told Seth something like, "make sure your butt is up and ready to go."

Even though it was late, Garth called Katy Monroe. From what Garth said afterward, Katy was ready and willing to come over in the morning. He also said she had badgered him earlier about going along on the trip to the Gator Lagoon, but to no avail.

When all of the calls were completed, the three of us sat at the kitchen table and took turns going to the refrigerator for refills of beer. We also took turns going to the bathroom.

After a few beers, my appetite started to return. I remembered we put the sandwiches we had brought into Garth's refrigerator before we left. During the drive to Garth's, Frankie and I had absent-mindedly munched on some of the snacks, but we didn't have much of a craving for food. And when we first arrived at Garth's, it was too stressful for any of us to eat.

I grabbed the three sandwiches and handed them out around the table. For all of us, the same eating pattern took place. After several slow—almost forced—bites, the hunger urge kicked in and we all finished our sandwiches with a flourish.

During one of Garth's trips to pee, Frankie lowered his voice and asked me what had happened when I was knocked down during our getaway. I told him that, to the best of my knowledge, Garth had broken the guard's neck.

Frankie drank more beers than I had ever seen him put away in one sitting. He was doing his best to calm down. We all were. The classical music on the radio provided a soothing background. It was a scene in striking contrast to the mayhem that had transpired earlier. There were some periods of time when none of us spoke. But there were also a few toasts to our health along the way.

19

In the morning there was coffee, some bagels Garth had on hand, and showers around. We also worked on some of the bottles of spring water Frankie and I had brought. It was a fresh start for all of us. Plus, the anticipation of the whole group getting together helped energize the atmosphere.

Frankie completed his computer work with the video in no time. Otherwise, he was moving kind of slowly, and he looked a little bit rough around the edges. Frankie was doing his best to rally back from some overindulgence with the beers. His light weight kept him from having much of a capacity for extended drinking. For sure, the late-night sandwich he had eaten saved him from an even worse fate.

Katy Monroe arrived at twenty of eleven, and Seth and Gwen were not far behind. There was relieved and invigorated electricity in the air as friendly hugs were exchanged.

"Oh, Ben," said Gwen, as she held me close. She pulled back and, with several tears of joy on her face, said, "What happened to your nose? Your face looks red and bruised."

"I had a little spill," I said. "It's no big deal. I tripped on a mangrove root."

The hugs continued and crisscrossed until everyone had embraced everyone. Even Garth,

Frankie, and I traded grabs. The tone was quick to become businesslike when Frankie called us all to the kitchen table.

"On Garth's laptop," said Frankie, "I am going to play back what we recorded last night."

Before Frankie got the video rolling, I turned to Gwen and whispered, "You may not want to watch this. It was Evan Montgomery from your department."

"No," she said. "Oh, no."

As Frankie played the video, which also had remarkably good audio, we all watched and listened. Gwen included. It was like seeing a terrible tragedy on the news, and not being able to keep your eyes off of it. The viewing was gruesome for those at the table who had not been there; but it was equally, or exceedingly, upsetting for me. I could tell Frankie was feeling the same way.

"Okay, Katy," said Frankie, when the video ended, "here are two memory sticks. You might need to have an extra one at some point. Each of them has what we just watched. There's one for you, Ben. And Garth, it is saved here on your laptop."

"What am I sucking hind tit here?" said Seth.

"If you want it," said Frankie, "I'll send it to you when we get home. I think the less actual memory sticks we have, the better."

"I think," said Katy, "this is the time to contact my friend who is the Assistant Chief of Police over on Sanibel. We have the evidence now. Let's get the ball rolling."

As Katy scrolled through her phone number file, she said, "His name is Mark Pendleton. I have told you that I've known him since high school. I'm going to put my phone on speaker, so you all can hear, but I think it is a good idea if you don't say anything. I have no intention of mentioning any of your names. At least, not yet."

We all listened quietly. After Katy and Mark Pendleton exchanged opening pleasantries, Katy said, "Mark, I have video, along with audio, of a murder that occurred last night in the Ding Darling Wildlife Refuge."

"What?" said Pendleton.

"Yes," said Katy, "and it was carried out, execution-style, by the heads of a bank that is secretly located in the refuge. It is not the first time this very thing has happened. I have reliable sources who have witnessed it previously. I am going to email the tape to you for evidence. Should I use the main contact address at the police department?"

"Ah, no," said Pendleton. "That puts it through too much red tape. I can get to it much quicker if you send it to me at MPendleton@gmail.com. And, Katy, I can't thank you enough for this."

"You will be getting back to me with the progress of the investigation, Mark?" asked Katy. "This is going to be a big article for me to write for the News-Press. I'd like updates as you can supply them."

"No problem, Katy," said Pendleton. "I'm thinking we may have to put together a task force for this. It sounds big. I have a feeling Monday morning it will be happening. I'll keep you informed. For now, you can consider yourself the sole media outlet. As things go on, that will expand, of course."

"Thanks, Mark," said Katy.

"No," he said, "thank you."

After the conversation ended, there seemed to be a relieved feeling fall over us all. The issue was now in the hands of the police, which was a definite upgrade from what had, to that point, only been a vigilante uprising by our small group. With smiles on all of our faces, more hugs of relief were passed around.

It occurred to me we had not told Katy everything that transpired the night before. With a serious tone to my voice, I said, "Katy, there is one more thing we need to tell you. There was more than one casualty last night."

"Really?" said Katy.

Before I could speak, Garth interrupted, saying, "Katy, I killed one of the security guards from The Bank when we were getting out of there. No sense going into detail. Let's put it this way, it was a matter of life or death."

"As shrewd as The Bank is," said Frankie, "I am not so sure they would want anybody on the outside to know about it anyway. They wouldn't want the attention raised."

"The guard just disappeared," said Seth. "Heck, they might just dispose of him in that Gator Lagoon."

"Look," said Katy, "thanks for telling me. As far as I am concerned, this is side information and it doesn't need to become public. I am sure it was something that had to be done. In effect, you did away with a murderer. I'm just glad it wasn't one of you guys."

Katy made a hasty exit to go home so she could compile the information. It was easy to see she was excited about being ready to file a blockbuster report as the story developed.

Garth suggested Woody's, up the canal, for lunch. The rest of us agreed, and I said we would be driving the short distance to the bar. I knew Gwen and I were riding back home together in my Jeep, and I didn't want any problems with leaving Woody's to ride back in Garth's boat.

Frankie chimed in that he thought driving was a good idea, too. He and Seth would take Garth with them in Seth's van, and bring him back. I could see Frankie was trying to remove at least one layer of delay when it came to corralling Seth and heading home. Especially on this day, since it was clear that Frankie wasn't feeling so great. I doubted he was up to doing any beer drinking at all.

We met at Woody's and sat at a table on the deck in the shade. Each of us enjoyed fish sandwiches with all the fixings. After relaxing and listening to a few songs by the day's live musician, Gwen and I decided to take off. Seth announced he would not take any money from us for the lunch. He then became insistent when I pressed the issue. With firmness, Seth said it was his treat for everyone and there would be no exceptions.

The drive home with Gwen was a pleasant

cruise. It was a Saturday in mid-September, the quietest month of the year for extra traffic. School had started, so there was practically no tourist traffic, local or otherwise. Plus, it was not a workday. Gwen and I did not talk much during the ride, but she rubbed my shoulder and neck off and on.

As we were driving over the Sanibel Causeway, Gwen said, as a statement, "So you were the one who was the case of life or death."

"Who told you that?" I asked.

"I think you just did," she said. "Oh, Ben, Ben, Ben. What am I going to do with you? This stuff has got to stop."

"Right," I said. "The cops have got it now."

"That is a relief," said Gwen, as she ran her fingers up the back of my head and grabbed onto my hair.

As we went up Periwinkle, I started to envision what things would be like after The Bank was no longer in existence. It seemed as though my adult life was starting all over again. And I didn't have any apprehensions of what lay ahead. I felt as though, if I hung onto Gwen, anything was possible. And it would be good.

We got back to the house and made a beeline to my bedroom. The next hour or more was filled with such a blaze of love that it seemed to flash by in an instant. What followed was probably a similar length of time Gwen and I held each other close and catnapped.

Around five-thirty, we went downstairs to see Frankie and Seth sitting in the living room. The television was on, but they were both staring into space with completely vacant looks on their faces. They seemed to be in some form of shock.

"Hey," I said, "is everything okay with you guys? Nothing bad happened, did it?"

"Yeah," said Frankie, "something bad happened. You better sit down for this one."

"You are not going to fucking believe this, Bennie," said Seth.

"What is it?" I asked. "What the hell is it?"

Frankie turned toward Gwen and me saying, "The cop on Sanibel who Katy called is in with *them*. I don't know what made me do this when we got home about an hour ago. But I checked the recording from the bugs we have in Farr's office and the conference room to see if there was any fallout from last night. Pendleton has already gone to Farr with the video."

"No," Gwen and I said in unison.

"Yes," said Frankie. "Listen to this. It's only the two of them talking."

"This had to happen in the last couple of hours," I said.

"Right," said Frankie. "Check it out."

"Bastards," said Seth.

Farr: I appreciate you contacting me, Assistant Chief Pendleton, so that we could meet this afternoon. You brought the video with you?

Pendleton: Yes, sir. I have saved it to this memory stick. The quality of the video and sound is amazingly good. And, as you will see, the date and time of day is noted in the lower right-hand corner of the recording.

Farr: Let me install it on my computer and take a look.......The quality of this video is, indeed, very good. Assistant Chief Pendleton, there was a necessary procedure which took place last night to ensure the continued security of The Bank. It was conducted with all normal precautions in place, and was viewed in person only by employees with proper clearance. As you had mentioned earlier on the phone, this was supplied to you by a reporter who is with one of the main local media outlets. Do you believe this person was responsible for filming the video?

Pendleton: No, sir, I do not believe my source was involved in the actual filming. The reporter and I have known each other for many years. Additionally, this person was supplied the film by an unnamed third party whose identity was not divulged. And there is every reason to expect an ensuing law enforcement inquiry. I am merely alerting you in advance, so you will be prepared. I am holding off from opening the investigation until Monday morning.

Farr: Very good, sir. I am thankful for your input and for your sustained assistance in maintaining the interests of The Bank. The contents of this envelope I am giving you serve as an additional supplement to your usual stipend. I trust you will keep me abreast of any further developments as the investigation goes along. That is all for now.

Pendleton: Yes, sir.

"Oh, man," I said.

"Yeah," said Frankie, "but that's not all. Listen to what was on the tape that Seth and I heard a few minutes ago. There was a quick meeting called, and it just ended. It didn't last long, but it is deep."

Farr: Fellow Fraternal Members, there is an urgency that exists for us all, and for the future of The Bank. I have been supplied with a video, including sound, of last night's cleansing assembly. The source of said video is unknown, although it would not surprise me if it came from our very ranks.......A police investigation will be launched on Monday morning. Therefore, it is necessary for the survival of The Bank, and for the continued existence of our Fraternal Brotherhood, to take bold steps. Ms. Branstein, contact our pilot at Page Field and instruct him to file a flight plan for our corporate jet. Make it a nine-o'clock departure this evening to Andros Island.

Branstein: Yes, sir.

Farr: Mr. Dunn, to protect our safety, see to it that you incorporate sufficient arms in your belongings.

Dunn: Always, sir.

Farr: The six of us in this room will be making this necessary flight. We are the Fraternal Brotherhood. It is an essential transition for us and for future opportunities in support of The Bank. The emergency protocol will be followed. Upon our arrival on Andros Island, we will each be provided with sufficient credentials to assume new identities. We will then proceed to travel separately. Each of us will ferry ample funds. The ultimate destination where we will reconvene will be revealed upon our arrival on Andros Island. We will not be deterred in our mission to dominate the world's financial markets. We are the Fraternal Members, and we will prevail.

Multiple voices: Yes, sir.

Farr: WAIN, Mr. Dunn?

Dunn: Whatever action is necessary, sir.

Farr: We will gather here at eight-o'clock. One suitcase and one smaller bag per person. Be sure to include ceremonial robes in your luggage. Ms. Branstein, contact our driver and have him prepare the company limousine for a trip to Page Field. Fraternal Members, we have a destiny with fortune and we will not be denied. Hail, Fraternal Members.

Multiple voices: Hail, Fraternal Members.

As Frankie was turning off the tape, his cell phone rang. With a blank look on his face, he answered it saying, "Yes, Ms. Branstein…yes…I will have the limo ready…yes."

Frankie disconnected the call, looked up, and said, "Guess what just got dropped in my lap?"

20

Several minutes of silence followed, until Seth said, "We've got to stop them. We can't let those bastards get away."

"The problem is," I said, "we don't have the cops with us at this point. I've got to call Garth. For one thing, I have to let him know about Katy's so-called friend."

"I wonder how long that guy has been on the take," said Seth.

"Maybe," said Gwen, "Katy could have some pull with the police over in Fort Myers and get them on the case."

"Look," said Frankie, "it's five-thirty. I have to be over there at the complex and have the limo ready to go in a couple of hours. I don't know how much progress Katy or anybody else could make with the cops in that short a time. It's a video. It's not a live smoking gun. The cops would probably be taking a little while to be sure about what supposedly happened, before they detain a bunch of hotshot corporate types from taking off on a business trip. Might not make for very good publicity."

As the others bantered about the situation, I called Garth. The lunch at Woody's must have ended not long after Gwen and I left, because Garth was clearly not affected by excessive drinking. To my surprise, I had noticed that was true for Seth, too.

Garth said he would call Katy to break the news, and then call back.

I hung up and sat back down next to Gwen. "We have to give this as much time as possible," I said. "Just hoping Katy can somehow make progress with the police. We have to go to Page Field and see if we can do anything to delay them from leaving."

Frankie perked up and said, "We can use the ear bud radio transmitters we used when we planted the bugs. At least we can keep in touch on the drive over to Page Field. Keep in mind the plane will be leaving from the new terminal that just opened. It's a Saturday night in September. Traffic won't be bad at all. It will take maybe forty-five minutes to get there."

"Maybe less," said Seth, "if they tell you to put the hammer down on the accelerator."

"I doubt that will happen," said Frankie. "They probably won't want to be getting any attention from the cops."

"Okay," I said, "here is what we will do. There are four ear buds for the radio system. All four of us will be wearing one. While Frankie is picking up his precious cargo at The Bank compound, the three of us will leave here in Seth's van. We ought to travel a few minutes ahead of the limo. That way we'll get to Page Field first. I'll tell Garth to meet us there."

"Let's do it," said Gwen. "We have to."

Garth called back on my cell phone and said he would be waiting in the parking lot at Page Field. Katy was already on her way to the headquarters building of the Fort Myers Police Department. Garth said she planned to occupy the main office and browbeat everyone in sight until she got some action.

The two hours until Frankie was leaving for The Bank fell under the category of *hurry up and wait*. Frankie took a shower and dressed, but Gwen, Seth, and I pretty much just milled around with nervous energy. More than fearfulness, I think we were all anxious for things to happen. Since I'd only had two beers at lunch, which was many hours prior, I addressed the driving issue with Seth. With very little resistance, he agreed to let me drive his van. He probably was fine in regard to the beer consumption, but he freely admitted that he'd had a good deal more than me.

As the minutes crawled along, I had several fleeting flashbacks to the first night at the Gator Lagoon. Although it had happened before, the frequency of the momentary frozen images had lessened in the past several weeks. Witnessing a second horrible event the night before was probably what triggered a recurrence in me. Not to mention seeing it all over again on the video, with sound no less. Still photographs in vivid color with bright spotlights, flaming torches, all the participants, including the ill-fated victim, burst into my mind's eye. Maybe it was providing motivation for me, but I tried my best to shake it off.

With all of the stress, none of us had been hungry. But Gwen rifled through the refrigerator and the cabinets and came up with a paper bag of modest snack material. Seth had the foresight to pack a cooler of beer for what he, no doubt, envisioned as a triumphant ride home. I added some bottles of spring water on top of the beer.

We each put in the single ear bud and did a test run on the four-way radio system. Everything was working fine. It was hard to believe that less than a whisper was audible to the other three of us. I suggested we have minimal talking in the van on our trip to Page Field. What was going on in the limousine with Frankie at the wheel was of primary importance. Plus, the conversation of the others in the limo would be able to be heard if none of us were making a sound.

Just after seven-thirty, Frankie left in his Camaro to drive over to the compound. It was a nervous twenty minutes in the air-conditioning until the three of us came out of the house. I got behind the wheel of the van, and Seth sat next to me as my co-pilot. Behind us, Gwen took a seat in the lounge chair that was usually reserved for Seth to be carted home in when the guys went out.

None of us spoke a word for minutes until Frankie whispered, "The cars are rolling in."

I started the van and we made our way down to Wildlife Drive and out to Sanibel-Captiva Road. There were no problems with traffic as we drove to the causeway. But it was the eeriest thing for the three of us to be riding along in silence. There was no apparent conversation in the limo until I was guiding the van off the causeway bridge and onto the mainland.

In the lowest of whispers, Frankie said, "There's a security guard with us."

Quiet followed until in the ear bud was the voice of Ava Branstein making a phone call. It was to the pilot of the corporate jet at Page Field. When she finished the conversation, she announced to the other passengers, "To quote our pilot in his aviation vernacular, he said, 'you've got a clean bird, and we're good to go.' The man certainly has a way with words."

As we drove up Summerlin, the sun was going down behind us. But ahead, a dark line of thunderstorms crossed our path. Just as we passed under the flyover at Gladiolus, it began to rain hard. When we crossed through the Cypress Lake intersection, Frankie whispered lightly into the radio, "Just cresting the causeway bridge."

"Rain up ahead for you," I said. "Just drove into it after Gladiolus."

By the time we got to the right bend onto Boy Scout Drive, the rain lightened. And in the short distance across 41 to the terminal at Page Field, it stopped altogether. When we pulled into the parking lot, I could see Garth's white pickup in the fading daylight.

We parked next to Garth, and I immediately went to him to quietly explain that the three of us, and also Frankie, were wearing radio transmitters. Seconds later, Frankie said at a barely audible level, "We'll be bringing the limo through the side gate directly onto the tarmac. You can't go in that way, go through the terminal. We're in the rain now."

"The rain stops when you are on Boy Scout," I said.

The four of us still had no plan of what to do as we walked to the terminal building. Before we got to the glass double-doors, I stopped us, saying, "If anybody asks, just act like we're waiting for someone."

When we went inside, a Port Authority officer was talking to a younger guy who was sitting behind the main desk. Other than the two of them, the terminal was empty. The airport employee called out, "Can I help you folks?"

"Thanks," I said. "We're waiting to meet a friend. Thought we would take a look around at the beautiful facility you have here."

"No problem," he said. "Take as long as you want. We don't lock the doors until eleven. There is a flight taking off soon, if you want to watch. Just go out through that other set of glass doors."

"Thanks," I said, as we walked out. A short distance across the tarmac sat The Bank's Gulfstream G280 jet with its engines warming. Even at idle, they made quite a bit of noise. Frankie had been right about the plane. It was the fanciest piece of aircraft I had ever seen. The pilot was making the rounds of his pre-flight checklist.

Within minutes, Frankie whispered again, "Pulling into the parking lot. Going to the side gate. Port Authority cop will be letting us in."

Seth, Gwen, and I turned and looked at each other with frozen stares. I said, "Where did Garth go?"

It was almost completely dark, and the outside lights on the terminal building were on. We looked in every direction, but no sign of Garth anywhere. At low speed, the limousine came through the side gate and rolled to a stop not far from the jet.

I motioned for Gwen to move back toward the doors of the terminal as the passengers were getting out of the limo. The group consisted of Lucien Farr, Ava Branstein, Webb Dunn, Harris Copeland, and two other high-level managers. As Frankie went around and opened the trunk, the security guard from The Bank who had ridden with them stepped away and observed the activity.

The Port Authority officer had closed the side gate behind the limo and was walking past us back to the terminal building. Because of the lighting and the distance we were from the limo, Seth and I had yet to be recognized. I turned to him and said, "Well, it's now or never."

The group was unloading their luggage from the trunk as I strode toward them with Seth a step off my shoulder. "Hold on there," I called. As all of their faces turned toward us, I could hear Ava Branstein over the din of the jet engines say, "It's Bennett Stradley and Stanton's son."

I continued, "The police will be here any minute. It's no use trying to leave."

The Bank's security guard pulled his firearm and aimed it toward Seth and me. "Stand back," he yelled. With that, Garth flashed out of the surrounding shadows and delivered a blow to the guard from behind. He went to the ground and lay motionless as his gun skidded away toward the limo.

Webb Dunn pulled his own handgun and fired several shots in Garth's direction as he retreated in zigzag fashion back into the shadows. In the same instant, I realized Seth had turned back toward the terminal. At the sound of the shots, the Port Authority officer, who had yet to reach the building, wheeled around with his pistol in hand. Seth tackled him to the ground and took his weapon from him.

The management group of The Bank scurried up the steps of the jet with luggage in hand. Webb Dunn was bringing up the rear in covering their escape. Seth got up and sprinted toward where I was crouching down. He was aiming the gun and yelling for them to stop when Dunn leveled his firearm and blasted off two shots that tore into Seth's upper torso. He dropped in his tracks only a few feet from me. In the light from the terminal I could see blood gushing from Seth's chest.

I looked toward the limo to see Frankie taking cover behind the side of it. He scooted on his hands and knees to retrieve the gun Garth had knocked away from the security guard. Frankie picked it up and it jammed as he tried to shoot at Webb Dunn going up the steps of the plane. Dunn turned as he was going through the airplane door and fired a single shot that caught Frankie in his upper body and spun him to the ground.

I raced over to him as the jet taxied away. I could see the bullet had hit him in his left shoulder, away from any organs. Frankie was bleeding, but not like Seth. I peeled my shirt off and pressed down firmly on the wound.

"You're going to be okay, Frankie," I said. "We're going to get help."

"What about Seth?" asked Frankie, grimacing in pain.

"Not good," I said.

Gwen was screaming in a wail as she ran out of the terminal toward us. Garth was right on her heels.

"Ben," said Frankie, "the limo is the only weapon we've got. Get it going toward the plane down at the end of the runway. The cruise setting is at the end of the right lever. Push it in and roll out of the car."

I jumped into the driver's seat of the limo just before Gwen and Garth reached me. As they approached, I could hear Gwen calling, "No, Ben.

No, Ben."

I didn't realize the car had been sitting at idle, and I screeched the starter when I turned the key to the ignition. As I pulled away I saw Garth grab Gwen in a bear hug to stop her.

The jet had taxied the short distance to the western end of the runway near 41. It did not hesitate as it turned and fired up its engines. I floored the gas on the limo and steered it in an intersecting angle to the plane's path. As soon as I pressed in the cruise control setting, I opened the door and dove out. It was a painful landing as I tumbled onto the runway. I could feel a snap in my left leg, and my head bounced off the runway at least once. I also felt an intense burning sensation on my left arm and bare back. I leaned up to see the limo headed on a direct line toward the accelerating jet. The plane's tires had just barely come off the runway as the limo clipped them, cartwheeling the aircraft in an abrupt flip. The jet crashed to the runway with a violent explosion and an incredible ball of fire. The blast was deafening and blinding.

I think I was in and out of consciousness for the next few minutes. What I do remember hearing was Gwen's voice shrieking, "Ben, Ben." And in the background I heard sirens.

21

The last month has been rough in a number of ways. I have been recuperating from my laundry list of injuries at a slow pace. In no particular order, my broken leg has been in a cast from my hip all the way down. Since it was a nasty compound fracture, I have at least another month to go before it comes off. Plus, I've been woozy off and on from the concussion I sustained when my head hit the runway.

But my hearing is gradually improving from the blast of the explosion. I am sure the radio transmitter ear bud I was wearing amplified the damage. The first things to clear up were my two black eyes from the tumble to the ground when I was tackled in the wildlife refuge, and the road burns I got on my arm and back when I dove out of the limo.

Frankie is making modest progress in his recovery from the bullet wound to his shoulder. But worst of all, Seth was pronounced dead before the paramedics could even get him into an ambulance. By far, he had paid the biggest price of all. A young, strong, healthy friend was gone, just like that. It is difficult to think about. Frankie and I are constantly reminded though, as we deal with our injuries. It could just as easily have been one or both of us. And Gwen is reminded every time she even looks at either of us.

I guess you could say the silver lining of it all was that there were no survivors from the plane crash. The entire top tier of management at The Bank was wiped out. Seth would have been happy about that.

From what I've heard from Gwen and Garth, Page Field was descended upon by police, fire, and EMS vehicles. It was a combined effort by Fort Myers, Lee County, and Port Authority emergency personnel. I missed a good bit of that activity. My recall after the barrel roll onto the runway was, and still is, sketchy.

The guard from The Bank who Garth had knocked unconscious was taken into custody that night. And within a day, so was the entire security detail at The Bank's complex. During that same time, Assistant Chief of Police Pendleton on Sanibel was arrested for his participation.

Gwen told me that Frankie and I were each taken in our own personal ambulance to Lee Memorial Hospital, not many miles north on 41 in Fort Myers. Due to the nature of our injuries, we both were kept in the hospital for several days. Gwen was by my side practically the entire time, day and night. On a couple of occasions she was chased out of the room while the doctors and nurses went about their business with me. At those times, she went down the hall to visit Frankie.

Garth came and went during our stay at Lee Memorial. He and Gwen ate a few meals together downstairs in the cafeteria. My parents also made frequent visits.

On Monday morning, Frankie and I had surgical procedures. Frankie had the wound to his shoulder patched up upon arrival on Saturday night, but on Monday the surgeons fine-tuned that work. My leg had several fractures that required surgery before being put in the cast. It was worth the wait for both of us to have the top-line surgeons performing the operations at the beginning of a new week.

Tuesday afternoon, Frankie and I were released. Garth had gotten the keys to Seth's van from the buttoned pocket of my cargo shorts. At first, it was like pulling teeth with the nurses to get access to the bag holding my clothes. Katy Monroe visited while Garth was there. She proceeded to stir things up enough with the staff to the point where they relented and let Garth have the keys.

Garth drove to Page Field and returned to the hospital with Seth's van. It was apparent that his small pickup would not hold all four of us. Gwen and I piled in the back of the van and I stretched out with the cumbersome cast on my leg as best I could. Garth drove us back to Page Field with Frankie at his side up front.

Even though it was a bright afternoon, there was a veil of gloominess, which wouldn't normally be associated with such a nice day. I knew we were all feeling it. Pulling into the parking lot and return-ing to the scene of the carnage was a distressing experience. Garth turned the keys to the van over to Gwen, and he bid us goodbye before driving off in his pickup. There wasn't much parting conversation, although Garth did make a point to hug each of us. I think everyone wanted to be gone from Page Field.

At one point during the ride to Sanibel, I looked over and saw Seth's cooler. I reached down and lifted the lid to see eight or ten beers and a few bottles of spring water lying in a bath of water from the melted ice. Seth had planned to put away a few on the way back Saturday night. What he foresaw as a triumphant ride home was anything *but* a triumphant one for us.

Katy had broken the story in the News-Press with only superficial details in Sunday morning's paper. She had a more in-depth report on Monday, and it had gone nationwide. She detailed all of the evils The Bank had been involved in.

Who knows what will happen to the facility on Andros Island. The Bahamas has a secretive policy with banks located on its soil, and there is no evidence to indicate anyone there played a part in the cold-blooded activity on Sanibel. Most likely, the pending investigation by international regulators will result in the seizing of the assets of The Bank.

One good outcome stemming from the local police investigation was that no other employees of The Bank have been charged with any crimes, except for the security force. None of our fathers or any other subordinates in each of the departments were deemed to have played a role in the multitude of ruthless acts carried out by The Bank. The bad part, or good part depending how you looked at it, was everyone found themselves out of a job.

Gwen has had little remorse concerning the death of her Uncle Harris. Even so, it was hard for her to inform her father of the details surrounding not only her uncle's demise, but of his involvement in the terrible acts that had been committed.

Gwen has been my guardian angel during my recovery. She has moved into the house, and has helped both Frankie and me in more ways than I can think of. Frankie has basically been limited to being a one-armed man. And, being on crutches, I barely qualify as the walking wounded. The concussion symptoms and the hearing impairment are just extra little touches to overcome.

During the recuperation period, the three of us have tried to be as upbeat as possible, but it has been easier said than done. Only when it has been necessary has there been any discussion of what happened the night at Page Field. There have been many periods of time when the three of us have sat in silence looking back and forth at each other with short-lived glances. It has been all new territory for each of us.

Gwen and I are in as loving a relationship as ever. I would say even more so. However, with my leg being incapacitated by the cast, we have had to be more creative in expressing our affection for each other. We both realize it is just a matter of time until the situation improves.

Garth is still Garth. Several times in the early stages of recovery he drove over to our house from St. James City to check up on us all. And last week-end, Frankie, Gwen, and I made the road trip to Pine Island and met up with Garth at Woody's for lunch. We decided meeting there was best, since it would be too cumbersome for me to make it in and out of his boat for the ride up the canal and back. Katy was there, too. It was a good time.

Without a doubt, the single most difficult thing any of us has had to face was Seth's funeral. It was held the following Saturday after he died, and was the saddest day of my life. The service was held at the Sanibel Community Church, located on Periwinkle just north of Casa Ybel Road. It is a rustic-looking church, which was fitting for Seth's character and personality.

Gwen chauffeured Frankie and me to the church in her Audi sedan. I sat in the back and stretched my left leg, in the full cast, across the rear seat. Frankie rode shotgun. I don't think there was anything but short, one-syllable exchanges on the ten-minute ride. For the most part we were all quiet.

The three of us sat with Garth who was already in a pew. Katy Monroe came in a little later and joined our group. My parents and Frankie's parents came in together. We exchanged waves with them as they walked by to sit behind Seth's family at the front.

During the service, there was a universal display of emotion throughout the congregation. Especially from an inordinate number of single young women who were in attendance. Seth had made many acquaintances within the female population of Southwest Florida, and it showed.

Frankie delivered the eulogy, arm in sling and all. He was eloquent in his remarks, and hesitated only a few times to gather himself. By interspersing several humorous stories, he broke the strain everyone was feeling. It seemed there wasn't anyone who didn't benefit from the breaks of subtle laughter. Seth, and the way he lived his life, provided Frankie ample fodder to work with in relating the lighter anecdotes. It was a good thing Frankie curtailed his remarks to exclude some even funnier stories, which would have been inappropriate for the setting.

The surprise of the service was when Garth walked to the front of the church and strapped on an acoustic guitar that had been out of sight in the choir area. He proceeded to perform as soulful and deepfelt a rendition as you could imagine in singing the hymn, Higher Ground. Garth's gravelly voice and slow, methodical pace riveted everyone's attention. His performance came as a total shocker for those of us who knew him. It was a shame it took Seth's funeral to bring Garth's hidden talent out of its shell.

There was no graveside service because Seth had been cremated. But the entire gathering was invited to Seth's parents' house for a reception following the ceremony. Garth suggested Katy leave her car at the church and ride with him. They got in his pickup and followed behind us. It was a sad procession that slowly made its way up Sanibel-Captiva Road to The Sanctuary, and the Stantons' house.

Considering it was the latter part of September, and normally still hot, it was a beautiful, mild day with a light breeze. Puffy white clouds dotted the cobalt blue sky. The reception was held behind the Stantons' house on an expansive flagstone patio, which surrounded a large rectangular swimming pool. Mature oak trees outlined the area and provided ample shade.

The young female contingent of mourners was a diverse assortment of shapes and sizes, each with the common trait of displaying a slightly-less-than refined appearance. With practically all of them in abbreviated dresses, they fit the mold of what Seth's preferences were when it came to women. However, they did serve as a distraction for all. Several groups of more mature women intermittently stole somewhat condescending glances at the group of twenty-somethings. Those looks were in direct contrast to the perky gawks the young gals were getting from the older men.

Our group of five located an open table and took seats. Since it had only been a week after Frankie and I had sustained our injuries, neither of us was up to extended time on our feet. Especially me.

When Garth returned to the table with a tray of drinks for all of us, Katy turned to him, saying, "When I did that interview with you a few years ago, you never mentioned anything about your musical talents. I had no idea you played guitar and sang."

"Neither did the rest of us," I said. "I never even saw a guitar at your place any of the times I've been there."

"You were great," said Katy, as we all chimed in with overlapping compliments.

"Thanks," said Garth, "I just keep the guitar up in my loft, beside my bed. I have times at night when I can't sleep, so I sit up and play a few tunes.

Seems to help me relax. Guess it's happened often enough and long enough to where I've gotten better at it."

"I'll say," said Katy. "You remind me of Tom Waits."

Frankie, Gwen, and I took quick looks back and forth in complete unfamiliarity with who Katy was talking about.

"Tom Waits?" I asked.

"Yeah," said Katy, "Tom Waits. He has won a couple of Grammys and he just got inducted into the Rock and Roll Hall of Fame. Tom Waits has a voice a lot like Garth's."

"Well," said Garth, "maybe you ought to say I might have a voice sort of like his. I'm an amateur. He's big-time."

"Well, anyway," I said, "you ought to display your talents. I bet you could get a part-time gig on the weekends at Woody's or someplace like it."

"Aw," said Garth, "I don't know. I just like playing and singing for fun. Never thought about trying to make any money at it."

"Well, it could happen," said Gwen.

"Sure could," said Frankie.

My father walked across the patio to us from where the parents were gathered. He acknowledged Gwen first, having previously met her in the hospital. After he shook hands with Frankie, and told him what a great job he did with the eulogy, I introduced him to Katy and Garth.

Shaking Garth's hand, my father said, "I really enjoyed your music. It was the highlight of the service. And I want to express my gratitude for what you have done to help my son and his friends."

"Thank you, sir," said Garth. I was almost expecting Garth to call him chum.

"Beyond that," said my father, "I want to tell all of you how proud I am of your courage, and of what you did. It is a terrible shame what happened to Seth. The whole situation that led to it, everything about it, is disgusting. Entirely disgusting."

I could see my father was getting a little choked up with emotion as he cut the conversation short and walked away.

After he left, we all nibbled on tasty snacks, but there was a somber pall over the gathering, and for good reason. The refreshments would have been much more enjoyable had we been together for a different occasion.

During the course of our stay, and when we were all leaving, I couldn't help but notice Garth and Katy seeming to become closer. They had been casual friends for quite a while, but their attraction toward each other appeared to have taken a step forward. Maybe something positive could come out of all the strife everyone had been through, I thought.

As the legal investigation of the case wore on, each of us had to give statements to the police. Garth had already established a reliable reputation with numerous law enforcement and public safety agencies through his years in the area. Katy told Frankie, Gwen, and me that she had vouched for each of us during her conversations with the investigating officers.

Still in all, it was a stressful experience to go in one-by-one to answer questions and interact with a mix of Sanibel, Fort Myers, and Lee County police. There was even a faction of F.B.I. agents milling around and listening. It reminded me of witnesses being questioned in a stark, insolated room on television shows. But it was something we all carried out as best we could.

Toward the end of my session, one of the officers suggested that the next time any of us wanted to catch the bad guys we ought to wait for the police to handle the situation. I nodded back in a sheepish manner, but then added something like, "We were afraid you guys weren't going to make it in time… we couldn't let them get away."

Katy kept the rest of us up to date on the progress of the recovery operation that was undertaken at the Gator Lagoon. The alligators were removed from the general vicinity and the water in the low-lying area was drained. Evidence was found, which included multiple skeletal remains I am sure the forensic experts had a field day examining. Positive identification was made on Tyler Morrison and Evan Montgomery.

Serving as a point of closure for Garth, the investigation also identified remains of his uncle. It allowed their family to mark a ceremony in his honor. To put an exclamation point on the callous nature of The Bank, they also found what was left of the security guard who Garth had killed. Seth's earlier speculation of what might happen had been correct.

Through Katy, we heard that two additional

sets of remains had been recovered, but there had not yet been any positive identification for either. Word was that the body parts still being examined appeared to be much more decomposed than the others. The Bank must have been carrying out its "cleansing assemblies" for longer than any of us knew.

Thinking back on the events of the last several months has been overwhelming. Yes, everyone who worked at The Bank had been making a ridiculous amount of money. But now it was clear we had been living a lie all along. The required secretiveness, in so many ways, was false testament to what we thought we had been accomplishing. We had been serving a purpose that, in the end result, was evil. It was a welcome relief to have the scourge lifted.

Getting over Seth will not be easy. His vitality and almost larger-than-life presence made losing him hard to believe. There is going to be a void. I miss him more than I can say. There have been many times in the last weeks when I've been in the house and heard a noise outside. I look up almost expecting Seth to walk through the front door. It has been a depressing situation. The pain and the discomfort both Frankie and I have gone through physically seem easier to deal with than the loss of Seth.

For the surviving group of us, I do not know where it will all lead, but I do know what we did and the closer bond it established. Frankie, Garth, Gwen, and I will be forever linked together by the actions we had taken. And it is a good feeling.

I believe Gwen and I have a bright future together, and I am beyond happy about our prospects.

There is a unique sentiment I have toward Garth, which will never be underappreciated or forgotten. He stepped in on multiple occasions to help me when I was in danger. He saved my life. For sure, the same bright future Gwen and I share would not exist if it had not been for Garth.

Epilogue

Much has happened in the last three months. I can say with firm assurance that The Bank does not exist anymore...in any way. Aside from the elimination of the leadership group, and the incarceration of the security detail and the corrupt police officer, the assets of The Bank have been seized by international banking regulators.

Plus, the Ding Darling Wildlife Refuge has taken possession of the compound of buildings. They are planning on turning it into an environmental education center. The emphasis will be on youth, and the facility will be used for school field trips and vacation day camps. It will also be open on weekends for the general public. Refuge staff will be included, but the bulk of the teachers and guides will be senior citizen volunteers. Sounds like a win-win situation in every way.

Frankie has healed up well from his wound. He and his father have taken ownership of a shuttle and limousine service. Even though it tends to be a seasonal business, they feel good about the potential for success. They will be doing quite a bit of work at the Southwest Florida International Airport, along with contracting shuttle service with several lodgings on Sanibel and Captiva. Frankie loves to do the off and on double-duty as a mechanic and also as a driver. He has to stay busy.

We decided to give up the lease on the house on Dinkins Lake Road. Frankie moved in with two guys he was friends with in high school. They live in a house sitting right on the edge of the Fort Myers Country Club. It is a stylish rancher with some impressive palm trees. From the back of the house, the view looking out on the golf course is great.

Frankie's parents are in the process of selling their house in The Sanctuary. The plan is to move to Fort Myers and be closer to the shuttle business. Frankie heard that Seth's dad landed the food and beverage management position at a new country club opening near Naples. So they will be leaving Sanibel, too.

My parents have already sold their house in The Sanctuary. By way of previous contacts in the Philadelphia area, my father was hired by the owners of a large office complex to manage all of their facilities. The offices are located on the Main Line in Bryn Mawr, Pennsylvania. Two weeks ago, my parents moved to a house in nearby Villanova. They are right back in the same area where they both grew up and lived their whole lives, before Sanibel and The Bank.

From the group of parents' standpoint, dealing with what has changed in their lives should hopefully be a positive adjustment. But it sure won't be all that much of a comforting feeling for the Stantons. They lost their son in the process.

What a terrible shame for Seth to be gone. He was an individual unto himself. Even though he constantly wanted to have fun, he fully respected the value of being dependable and doing a good job. His personality was a cross between those two extremes. He will always be missed.

Frankie had updates about Katy and Garth. Just as Garth had suggested the first time I met her, Katy got a position with USA Today. Her work on the story of The Bank, and its demise, spring-boarded her to national prominence with the media. For now, she will be covering all of Florida as a lead journalist. It is a big jump from her days as a cub reporter with the weekly paper on Pine Island. She earned it.

The word is Garth and Katy have been spending more time together. Frankie said it's being portrayed as strictly a friendship-type relationship. But he has his doubts. Apparently, Garth has been traveling with Katy when reporting assignments take her around the state. He even had a hitch welded on the back of her Bronco to tow his fishing boat. No matter what the arrangement is between them, I feel sure it is good. They both have the same kind of practical and sensible approach to life.

Regardless of how things turn out with Garth and Katy, it is easy to tell they get along well as friends. That is the important part. With Garth's contractor status with the Florida Fish and Wildlife Conservation Commission, he will probably be able to pick up projects around the state to coincide with Katy's travel. One way or another, they will make a good team.

Garth. He is, without a doubt, the most unique and special person I have ever met. What a person to know. What a person to call your friend.

Little did I know when he plopped me down to the ground the first night I met him at the Gator Lagoon that he would become such a valued ally.

Gwen has had many lengthy phone conversations with each of her parents. Her father was so repulsed by the events leading to his brother's death that he didn't fly down for a memorial service, which was held a month or so later. Gwen's mother pressed her about coming down for a visit, but Gwen successfully held her off. She cited my recovery, and our awkward living arrangement as not making for the best circumstances.

Gwen and I did, however, pay them a visit for a couple of nights over the holidays at their house on Long Island. It was during our trek north to our new home. In early January, we moved to Saratoga Springs, New York. The same town where Gwen went to college at Skidmore.

Gwen has enrolled in the Masters program in Liberal Studies there. She is thinking she may want to teach at Skidmore, and even go on to get her doctorate. The big motivating factor of her whole pursuit is that she has been accepted as a volunteer graduate assistant for the women's riding team. Gwen has a very good relationship with both of the coaches. Throughout her four years, she was one of the best riders on the team. The head coach is nearing retirement, and it appears it could just be a matter of time before Gwen moves up to the assistant coach position.

For the spring semester, which starts near the end of January, we decided to rent an apartment near the Skidmore campus. It will give us a chance to look around and take our time in making any long-term choice of housing.

I like Saratoga Springs. It is a picturesque and appealing town. Old-fashioned, upstate New York. And the mountainous scenery in the surrounding area is stunning. Although we missed the changing of the leaves in the fall, Gwen said the colors are spectacular in October. Looking forward to seeing them later this year. It will be a different version of Mother Nature's beauty compared to the vivid sunsets over the Gulf of Mexico.

Since it is January, I have had to make some serious adjustments in acclimating to the effects of cold weather on my body. Even indoors, I've been layering on multiple sweatshirts. Gwen readapted to northern winters easily since she had only spent one summer on Sanibel. On the other hand, my two full years in Southwest Florida in the subtropical climate was long enough to transform, for the worse, the way I look at the cold. I grew up near Philadelphia, so I ought to know better. But it doesn't take very long to change your perception of comfort. I am working on it.

My injuries have healed to the point where I am getting around fairly well. Well enough to go on a job interview that turned out to be successful. Using contacts from her previous employment, Gwen set me up to meet with two of the facilities managers at the Saratoga Race Course. I hit it off great with both of them, and will be starting as a mid-level assistant at the beginning of May.

Because of the reduced activity at the track when there is no live racing, the off-season is quieter. It should be good timing for me to get familiar with the facilities. I see an opportunity for future advancement since both of the managers have been at Saratoga for close to thirty years.

It will be interesting working at the track. I don't know anything about horse racing, but I do know how to make sure a facility operates the way it ought to. I know I have a lot to learn, especially considering the age of many of the structures. I am looking forward to it.

Since I will have some available time until I start the new job, I am planning to go to Skidmore's home baseball games this spring. I may try to get my foot in the door with the coaching staff so that I could possibly help out with the team somewhere down the road. It would be great if Gwen and I both return to being involved on a regular basis with sports we each love.

Gwen and I are in the process of closing a chapter in our lives that has been particularly emotional in many ways. Overall, my time at The Bank had no specific setbacks. I had done my job, kept the secret, and made an outrageous amount of money—especially for someone who hadn't yet reached the age of twenty-five. At least Gwen spent only a matter of months doing something she didn't feel comfortable with.

We have already booked a flight during her spring break in late March. We are flying down to Florida to have a mini-reunion with Frankie, Garth, and Katy. It will be good to see them after some time has passed. Hoping we can all have some fun together. Both Gwen and I are looking forward to the trip. Aside from the excitement of seeing the rest of our team, I really can't wait for some warmer weather.

I called Garth the other day. He said he has picked up a part-time gig playing at Woody's on Sunday afternoons. He started sitting in with the acoustic guy, and it has turned into something a bit more regular. He is working it in with his travel schedule with Katy. I think it is great. We are already planning to catch Garth in action while we are down.

There will always be a soft spot in my heart for Sanibel. From a natural beauty standpoint, for me, it would be hard to top when compared to anywhere else to live or visit. It is as if the occupied half of Sanibel is just humbly sharing the island with the Ding Darling Wildlife Refuge. The island did not deserve to have The Bank casting a dark shadow on it.

Gwen and I are in love, and we look forward with optimism to our future together. But we have both pledged to never forget what happened. Everyday activities will overcome the memories to a point, but it will always be a part of us.

We have a brand new life ahead. As one, we are going to make sure the trip is an enjoyable journey.

Acknowledgements

To *Gayle Kasey*, whose vital assistance, in numerous aspects, has made this project possible

To *Gus Highfield*, for editorial assistance, coupled with valued advice and suggestions

To *Thomas Urech*, for sharing his knowledge of the banking industry

To *Dan Thompson*, for his knowledge of Sanibel Island

To *Chris Dowaliby*, for his familiarity with law enforcement practices

To *George Kasey*, for his knowledge of the aviation industry

To *Dave Kasey*, whose experiences helped provide a backdrop for the theme of this book